Crossroads of Destiny

AND OTHERS

Crossroads of Destiny

AND OTHERS

H. Beam Piper

ÆGYPAN PRESS

"Crossroads of Destiny" is reproduced from *Fantastic Universe Science Fiction,* July 1959.

"Hunter Patrol" is reproduced from *Amazing Stories,* May 1959.

"Dearest" is reproduced from *Weird Tales,* March, 1951.

"The Return" is reproduced from *The Science-Fictional Sherlock Holmes,* 1960.

"Rebel Raider" is reproduced from *True: The Man's Magazine,* December 1950.

Crossroads of Destiny and Others
A publication of
ÆGYPAN PRESS

www.aegypan.com

Table of Contents

Crossroads of Destiny 7

Hunter Patrol 17
A Collaboration with John J. McGuire

Dearest 45

The Return 61
A Collaboration with John J. McGuire

Rebel Raider 91

Crossroads of Destiny

I still have the dollar bill. It's in my box at the bank, and I think that's where it will stay. I simply won't destroy it, but I can think of nobody to whom I'd be willing to show it – certainly nobody at the college, my History Department colleagues least of all. Merely to tell the story would brand me irredeemably as a crackpot, but crackpots are tolerated, even on college faculties. It's only when they begin producing physical evidence that they get themselves actively resented.

When I went into the club-car for a nightcap before going back to my compartment to turn in, there were five men there, sitting together.

One was an Army officer, with the insignia and badges of a Staff Intelligence colonel. Next to him was a man of about my own age, with sandy hair and a bony, Scottish looking face, who sat staring silently into a highball which he held in both hands. Across the aisle, an elderly man, who could have been a lawyer or a banker, was smoking a cigar over a glass of port, and beside him sat a plump and slightly too well groomed individual who had a tall colorless drink, probably gin-and-tonic. The fifth man, separated from him by a vacant chair, seemed to be dividing his attention between a book on his lap and the conversation, in which he was taking no part. I sat down beside the sandy-haired man; as I did so and rang for the waiter, the colonel was saying:

"No, that wouldn't. I can think of a better one. Suppose you have Columbus get his ships from Henry the Seventh of England and sail under the English instead of the Spanish flag. You know, he did try to get English backing, before he went to Spain, but King Henry turned him down. That could be changed."

I pricked up my ears. The period from 1492 to the Revolution is my special field of American history, and I knew, at once, the enormous difference that would have made. It was a moment later that I realized how oddly the colonel had expressed the idea, and by that time the plump man was speaking.

"Yes, that would work," he agreed. "Those kings made decisions, most of the time, on whether or not they had a hangover, or what some court favorite thought." He got out a notebook and pen and scribbled briefly. "I'll hand that to the planning staff when I get to New York. That's Henry the Seventh, not Henry the Eighth? Right. We'll fix it so that Columbus will catch him when he's in a good humor."

That was too much. I turned to the man beside me.

"What goes on?" I asked. "Has somebody invented a time machine?"

He looked up from the drink he was contemplating and gave me a grin.

"Sounds like it, doesn't it? Why, no; our friend here is getting up a television program. Tell the gentleman about it," he urged the plump man across the aisle.

The waiter arrived at that moment. The plump man, who seemed to need little urging, waited until I had ordered a drink and then began telling me what a positively sensational idea it was.

"We're calling it *Crossroads of Destiny,*" he said. "It'll be a series, one half-hour show a week; in each episode, we'll take some historic event and show how history could have been changed if something had happened differently. We dramatize the event up to that point just as it really happened, and then a commentary-voice comes on and announces that this is the Crossroads of Destiny; this is where history could have been completely changed. Then he gives a résumé of what really did happen, and then he says, '*But* – suppose so and so had done this and that, instead of such and such.' Then we pick up the dramatization at that point, only we show it the way it might have happened. Like this thing about Columbus; we'll show how it could have happened, and end with Columbus wading ashore with his sword in one hand and a flag in the other, just like the painting, only it'll be the English flag, and Columbus will shout: 'I take possession of this new land in the name of His Majesty, Henry the Seventh of England!'" He brandished his drink, to the visible consternation of the elderly man beside him. "And then, the sailors all sing *God Save the King.*"

"Which wasn't written till about 1745," I couldn't help mentioning.

"Huh?" The plump man looked startled. "Are you sure?" Then he decided that I was, and shrugged. "Well, they can all shout, 'God Save King Henry!' or 'St. George for England!' or something. Then, at the end, we introduce the program guest, some history expert, a real name, and he tells how he thinks history would have been changed if it had happened this way."

The conservatively dressed gentleman beside him wanted to know how long he expected to keep the show running.

"The crossroads will give out before long," he added.

"The sponsor'll give out first," I said. "History is just one damn crossroads after another." I mentioned, in passing, that I taught the subject. "Why, since the beginning of this century, we've had enough of them to keep the show running for a year."

"We have about twenty already written and ready to produce," the plump man said comfortably, "and ideas for twice as many that the planning staff is working on now."

The elderly man accepted that and took another cautious sip of wine.

"What I wonder, though, is whether you can really say that history can be changed."

"Well, of course –" The television man was taken aback; one always seems to be when a basic assumption is questioned. "Of course, we only know what really did happen, but it stands to reason if something had happened differently, the results would have been different, doesn't it?"

"But it seems to me that everything would work out the same in the long run. There'd be some differences at the time, but over the years wouldn't they all cancel out?"

"Non, non, Monsieur!" the man with the book, who had been outside the conversation until now, told him earnestly. "Make no mistake; 'istoree can be shange'!"

I looked at him curiously. The accent sounded French, but it wasn't quite right. He was some kind of a foreigner, though; I'd swear that he never bought the clothes he was wearing in this country. The way the suit fitted, and the cut of it, and the shirt-collar, and the necktie. The book he was reading was Langmuir's *Social History of the American People* – not one of my favorites, a bit too much on the doctrinaire side, but what a bookshop clerk would give a foreigner looking for something to explain America.

"What do you think, Professor?" the plump man was asking me.

"It would work out the other way. The differences wouldn't cancel out; they'd accumulate. Say something happened a century ago, to throw a presidential election the other way. You'd get different people at the head of the government, opposite lines of policy taken, and eventually we'd be getting into different wars with different enemies at different times, and different batches of young men killed before they could marry and have families – different people being born or not being born. That would mean different ideas, good or bad, being advanced; different books written; different inventions, and different social and economic problems as a consequence."

"Look, he's only giving himself a century," the colonel added. "Think of the changes if this thing we were discussing, Columbus sailing under the English flag, had happened. Or suppose Leif Ericson had been able to plant a permanent colony in America in the Eleventh Century, or if the Saracens had won the Battle of Tours. Try to imagine the world today if any of those things had happened. One thing you can be sure of – any errors you make in trying to imagine such a world will be on the side of overconservatism."

The sandy-haired man beside me, who had been using his highball for a crystal ball, must have glimpsed in it what he was looking for. He finished the drink, set the empty glass on the stand-tray beside him, and reached back to push the button.

"I don't think you realize just how good an idea you have, here," he told the plump man abruptly. "If you did, you wouldn't ruin it with such timid and unimaginative treatment."

I thought he'd been staying out of the conversation because it was over his head. Instead, he had been taking the plump man's idea apart, examining all the pieces, and considering what was wrong with it and how it could be improved. The plump man looked startled, and then angry – timid and unimaginative were the last things he'd expected his idea to be called. Then he became uneasy. Maybe this fellow was a typical representative of his lord and master, the faceless abstraction called the Public.

"What do you mean?" he asked.

"Misplaced emphasis. You shouldn't emphasize the event that could have changed history; you should emphasize the changes that could have been made. You're going to end this show you were talking about with a shot of Columbus wading up to the beach with an English flag, aren't you?"

"Well, that's the logical ending."

"That's the logical beginning," the sandy-haired man contradicted. "And after that, your guest historian comes on; how much time will he be allowed?"

"Well, maybe three or four minutes. We can't cut the dramatization too short –"

"And he'll have to explain, a couple of times, and in words of one syllable, that what we have seen didn't really happen, because if he doesn't, the next morning half the twelve-year-old kids in the country will be rushing wild-eyed into school to slip the teacher the real inside about the discovery of America. By the time he gets that done, he'll be able to mumble a couple of generalities about vast and incalculable effects, and then it'll be time to tell the public about Widgets, the really safe cigarettes, all filter and absolutely free from tobacco."

The waiter arrived at this point, and the sandy-haired man ordered another rye highball. I decided to have another bourbon on the rocks, and the TV impresario said, "Gin-and-tonic," absently, and went into a reverie which lasted until the drinks arrived. Then he came awake again.

"I see what you mean," he said. "Most of the audience would wonder what difference it would have made where Columbus would have gotten his ships, as long as he got them and America got discovered. I can see it would have made a hell of a big difference. But how could it be handled any other way? How could you figure out just what the difference would have been?"

"Well, you need a man who'd know the historical background, and you'd need a man with a powerful creative imagination, who is used to using it inside rigorously defined limits. Don't try to get them both in one; a collaboration would really be better. Then you work from the known situation in Europe and in America in 1492, and decide on the immediate effects. And from that, you have to carry it along, step by step, down to the present. It would be a lot of hard and very exacting work, but the result would be worth it." He took a sip from his glass and added: "Remember, you don't have to prove that the world today would be the way you set it up. All you have to do is make sure that nobody else would be able to prove that it wouldn't."

"Well, how could you present that?"

"As a play, with fictional characters and a plot; time, the present, under the changed conditions. The plot – the reason the coward conquers his fear and becomes a hero, the obstacle to the boy marrying the girl, the reason the innocent man is being persecuted – will have to grow out of this imaginary world you've constructed, and be impossible in our real world. As long as you stick to that, you're all right."

"Sure. I get that." The plump man was excited again; he was about half sold on the idea. "But how will we get the audience to accept it? We're asking them to start with an assumption they know isn't true."

"Maybe it is, in another time-dimension," the colonel suggested. "You can't prove it isn't. For that matter, you can't prove there aren't other time-dimensions."

"Hah, that's it!" the sandy-haired man exclaimed. "World of alternate probability. That takes care of that."

He drank about a third of his highball and sat gazing into the rest of it, in an almost yogic trance. The plump man looked at the colonel in bafflement.

"Maybe this alternate-probability time-dimension stuff means something to you," he said. "Be damned if it does to me."

"Well, as far as we know, we live in a four-dimensional universe," the colonel started.

The elderly man across from him groaned. "Fourth dimension! Good God, are we going to talk about that?"

"It isn't anything to be scared of. You carry an instrument for measuring in the fourth dimension all the time. A watch."

"You mean it's just time? But that isn't –"

"We know of three dimensions of space," the colonel told him, gesturing to indicate them. "We can use them for coordinates to locate things, but we also locate things in time. I wouldn't like to ride on a train or a plane if we didn't. Well, let's call the time we know, the time your watch registers, Time-A. Now, suppose the entire, infinite extent of Time-A is only an instant in another dimension of time, which we'll call Time-B. The next instant of Time-B is also the entire extent of Time-A, and the next and the next. As in Time-A, different things are happening at different instants. In one of these instants of Time-B, one of the things that's happening is that King Henry the Seventh of England is furnishing ships to Christopher Columbus."

The man with the odd clothes was getting excited again.

"Zees – 'ow you say – zees alternate probabeelitay; eet ees a theory zhenerally accept' een zees countree?"

"Got it!" the sandy-haired man said, before anybody could answer. He set his drink on the stand-tray and took a big jackknife out of his pocket, holding it unopened in his hand. "How's this sound?" he asked, and hit the edge of the tray with the back of the knife, *Bong!*

"Crossroads – of – *Destiny!*" he intoned, and hit the edge of the tray again, *Bong!* "This is the year 1959 – but not the 1959 of our world, for we are in a world of alternate probability, in another dimension of time; a world parallel to and coexistent with but separate from our own, in which history has been completely altered by a single momentous event." He shifted back to his normal voice.

"Not bad; only twenty-five seconds," the plump man said, looking up from his wrist watch. "And a trained announcer could maybe shave five seconds off that. Yes, something like that, and at the end we'll have another thirty seconds, and we can do without the guest."

"But zees alternate probibeelitay, in anozzer dimension," the stranger was insisting. "Ees zees a concept original weet you?" he asked the colonel.

"Oh, no; that idea's been around for a long time."

"I never heard of it before now," the elderly man said, as though that completely demolished it.

"Zen eet ees zhenerally accept' by zee scienteest'?"

"Umm, no," the sandy-haired man relieved the colonel. "There's absolutely no evidence to support it, and scientists don't accept unsupported assumptions unless they need them to explain something, and they don't need this assumption for anything. Well, it would come in handy to make some of these reports of freak phenomena, like mysterious appearances and disappearances, or flying-object sightings, or reported falls of non-meteoric matter, theoretically respectable. Reports like that usually get the ignore-and-forget treatment, now."

"Zen you believe zat zeese ozzer world of zee alternate probabeelitay, zey exist?"

"No. I don't disbelieve it, either. I've no reason to, one way or another." He studied his drink for a moment, and lowered the level in the glass slightly. "I've said that once in a while things get reported that look as though such other worlds, in another time-dimension, may exist. There have been whole books published by people who collect stories like that. I must say that academic science isn't very hospitable to them."

"You mean, zings sometimes, 'ow-you-say, leak in from one of zees ozzer worlds? Zat has been known to 'appen?"

"Things have been said to have happened that might, if true, be cases of things leaking through from another time world," the sandy-haired man corrected. "Or leaking away to another time world." He mentioned a few of the more famous cases of unexplained mysteries – the English diplomat in Prussia who vanished in plain sight of a number of people, the ship found completely deserted by her crew, the lifeboats all in place; stories like that. "And there's this rash of alleged sightings of unidentified flying objects. I'd sooner believe that they came from another dimension than from another planet. But, as far as I know, nobody's seriously advanced this other-time-dimension theory to explain them."

"I think the idea's familiar enough, though, that we can use it as an explanation, or pseudo-explanation, for the program," the television man said. "Fact is, we aren't married to this Crossroads title, yet; we could just as easily all it *Fifth Dimension.* That would lead the public, to expect something out of the normal before the show started."

That got the conversation back onto the show, and we talked for some time about it, each of us suggesting possibilities. The stranger even suggested one – that the Civil War had started during the Jackson

Administration. Fortunately, nobody else noticed that. Finally, a porter came through and inquired if any of us were getting off at Harrisburg, saying that we would be getting in in five minutes.

The stranger finished his drink hastily and got up, saying that he would have to get his luggage. He told us how much he had enjoyed the conversation, and then followed the porter toward the rear of the train. After he had gone out, the TV man chuckled.

"Was that one an oddball!" he exclaimed. "Where the hell do you suppose he got that suit?"

"It was a tailored suit," the colonel said. "A very good one. And I can't think of any country in the world in which they cut suits just like that. And did you catch his accent?"

"Phony," the television man pronounced. "The French accent of a Greek waiter in a fake French restaurant. In the Bronx."

"Not quite. The pronunciation was all right for French accent, but the cadence, the way the word-sounds were strung together, was German."

The elderly man looked at the colonel keenly. "I see you're Intelligence," he mentioned. "Think he might be somebody up your alley, Colonel?"

The colonel shook his head. "I doubt it. There are agents of unfriendly powers in this country – a lot of them, I'm sorry to have to say. But they don't speak accented English, and they don't dress eccentrically. You know there's an enemy agent in a crowd, pick out the most normally American type in sight and you usually won't have to look further."

The train ground to a stop. A young couple with hand-luggage came in and sat at one end of the car, waiting until other accommodations could be found for them. After a while, it started again. I dallied over my drink, and then got up and excused myself, saying that I wanted to turn in early.

In the next car behind, I met the porter who had come in just before the stop. He looked worried, and after a moment's hesitation, he spoke to me.

"Pardon, sir. The man in the club-car who got off at Harrisburg; did you know him?"

"Never saw him before. Why?"

"He tipped me with a dollar bill when he got off. Later, I looked closely at it. I do not like it."

He showed it to me, and I didn't blame him. It was marked *One Dollar,* and *United States of America,* but outside that there wasn't a thing right about it. One side was grey, all right, but the other side was green. The picture wasn't the right one. And there were a lot of other things about it, some of them absolutely ludicrous. It wasn't counterfeit – it wasn't even an imitation of a United States bill.

And then it hit me, like a bullet in the chest. Not a bill of *our* United States. No wonder he had been so interested in whether our scientists accepted the theory of other time dimensions and other worlds of alternate probability!

On an impulse, I got out two ones and gave them to the porter – perfectly good United States Bank gold-certificates.

"You'd better let me keep this," I said, trying to make it sound the way he'd think a Federal Agent would say it. He took the bills, smiling, and I folded his bill and put it into my vest pocket.

"Thank you, sir," he said. "I have no wish to keep it."

Some part of my mind below the level of consciousness must have taken over and guided me back to the right car and compartment; I didn't realize where I was going till I put on the light and recognized my own luggage. Then I sat down, as dizzy as though the two drinks I had had, had been a dozen. For a moment, I was tempted to rush back to the club-car and show the thing to the colonel and the sandy-haired man. On second thought, I decided against that.

The next thing I banished from my mind was the adjective "incredible." I had to credit it; I had the proof in my vest pocket. The coincidence arising from our topic of conversation didn't bother me too much, either. It was the topic which had drawn him into it. And, as the sandy-haired man had pointed out, we know nothing, one way or another, about these other worlds; we certainly don't know what barriers separate them from our own, or how often those barriers may fail. I might have thought more about that if I'd been in physical science. I wasn't; I was in American history. So what I thought about was what sort of country that other United States must be, and what its history must have been.

The man's costume was basically the same as ours – same general style, but many little differences of fashion. I had the impression that it was the costume of a less formal and conservative society than ours and a more casual way of life. It could be the sort of costume into which ours would evolve in another thirty or so years. There was another odd thing. I'd noticed him looking curiously at both the waiter and the porter, as though something about them surprised him. The only thing they had in common was their race, the same as every other passenger-car attendant. But he wasn't used to seeing Chinese working in railway cars.

And there had been that remark about the Civil War and the Jackson Administration. I wondered what Jackson he had been talking about; not Andrew Jackson, the Tennessee militia general who got us into war with Spain in 1810, I hoped. And the Civil War; that had baffled me completely. I wondered if it had been a class-war, or a sectional conflict. We'd had plenty of the latter, during our first century, but all of them had been settled peacefully and Constitutionally. Well, some of the things he'd read in Lingmuir's *Social History* would be surprises for him, too.

And then I took the bill out for another examination. It must have gotten mixed with his spendable money – it was about the size of ours – and I wondered how he had acquired enough of our money to pay his train fare. Maybe he'd had a diamond and sold it, or maybe he'd had a gun and held somebody up. If he had, I didn't know that I blamed him, under the circumstances. I had an idea that he had some realization of what had happened to him – the book, and the fake accent, to cover any mistakes he might make. Well, I wished him luck, and then I unfolded the dollar bill and looked at it again.

In the first place, it had been issued by the United States Department of Treasury itself, not the United States Bank or one of the State Banks. I'd have to think over the implications of that carefully. In the second place, it was a silver certificate; why, in this other United States, silver must be an acceptable monetary metal; maybe equally so with gold, though I could hardly believe that. Then I looked at the picture on the grey obverse side, and had to strain my eyes on the fine print under it to identify it. It was Washington, all right, but a much older Washington than any of the pictures of him I had ever seen. Then I realized that I knew just where the Crossroads of Destiny for his world and mine had been.

As every schoolchild among us knows, General George Washington was shot dead at the Battle of Germantown, in 1777, by an English, or, rather, Scottish, officer, Patrick Ferguson – the same Patrick Ferguson who invented the breech-loading rifle that smashed Napoleon's armies. Washington, today, is one of our lesser national heroes, because he was our first military commander-in-chief. But in this other world, he must have survived to lead our armies to victory and become our first President, as was the case with the man who took his place when he was killed.

I folded the bill and put it away carefully among my identification cards, where it wouldn't a second time get mixed with the money I spent, and as I did, I wondered what sort of a President George Washington had made, and what part, in the history of that other United States, had been played by the man whose picture appears on our dollar bills – General and President Benedict Arnold.

THE END

Hunter Patrol

By H. BEAM PIPER *and* JOHN J. McGUIRE

At the crest of the ridge, Benson stopped for an instant, glancing first at his wrist-watch and then back over his shoulder. It was 0539; the barrage was due in eleven minutes, at the spot where he was now standing. Behind, on the long northeast slope, he could see the columns of black oil smoke rising from what had been the Pan-Soviet advance supply dump. There was a great deal of firing going on, back there; he wondered if the Commies had managed to corner a few of his men, after the patrol had accomplished its mission and scattered, or if a couple of Communist units were shooting each other up in mutual mistaken identity. The result would be about the same in either case – reserve units would be disorganized, and some men would have been pulled back from the front line. His dozen-odd UN regulars and Turkish partisans had done their best to simulate a paratroop attack in force. At least, his job was done; now to execute that classic infantry maneuver described as, "Let's get the hell outta here." This was his last patrol before rotation home. He didn't want anything unfortunate to happen.

There was a little ravine to the left; the stream which had cut it in the steep southern slope of the ridge would be dry at this time of year, and he could make better time, and find protection in it from any chance shots when the interdictory barrage started. He hurried toward it and followed it down to the valley that would lead toward the front – the thinly-held section of the Communist lines, and the UN lines beyond, where fresh troops were waiting to jump from their holes and begin the attack.

There was something wrong about this ravine, though. At first, it was only a vague presentiment, growing stronger as he followed the dry gully down to the valley below. Something he had smelled, or heard, or seen, without conscious recognition. Then, in the dry sand where the ravine debouched into the valley, he saw faint tank-tracks – only one pair.

There was something wrong about the vines that mantled one side of the ravine, too. . . .

An instant later, he was diving to the right, breaking his fall with the butt of his auto-carbine, rolling rapidly toward the cover of a rock, and as he did so, the thinking part of his mind recognized what was wrong. The tank-tracks had ended against the vine-grown side of the ravine, what he had smelled had been lubricating oil and petrol, and the leaves on some of the vines hung upside down.

Almost at once, from behind the vines, a tank's machine guns snarled at him, clipping the place where he had been standing, then shifting to rage against the sheltering rock. With a sudden motor-roar, the muzzle of a long tank-gun pushed out through the vines, and then the low body of a tank with a red star on the turret came rumbling out of the camouflaged bay. The machine guns kept him pinned behind the rock; the tank swerved ever so slightly so that its wide left tread was aimed directly at him, then picked up speed. Aren't even going to waste a shell on me, he thought.

Futilely, he let go a clip from his carbine, trying to hit one of the vision-slits; then rolled to one side, dropped out the clip, slapped in another. There was a shimmering blue mist around him. If he only hadn't used his last grenade, back there at the supply-dump. . . .

The strange blue mist became a flickering radiance that ran through all the colors of the spectrum and became an utter, impenetrable blackness. . . .

There were voices in the blackness, and a softness under him, but under his back, when he had been lying on his stomach, as though he were now on a comfortable bed. They got me alive, he thought; now comes the brainwashing!

He cracked one eye open imperceptibly. Lights, white and glaring, from a ceiling far above; walls as white as the lights. Without moving his head, he opened both eyes and shifted them from right to left. Vaguely, he could see people and, behind them, machines so simply designed that their functions were unguessable. He sat up and looked around groggily. The people, their costumes – definitely not Pan-Soviet uniforms – and the room and its machines, told him nothing. The hardness under his right hip was a welcome surprise; they hadn't taken his pistol from him! Feigning even more puzzlement and weakness, he clutched his knees with his elbows and leaned his head forward on them, trying to collect his thoughts.

"We shall have to give up, Gregory," a voice trembled with disappointment.

"Why, Anthony?" The new voice was deeper, more aggressive.

"Look. Another typical reaction; retreat to the fœtus."

Footsteps approached. Another voice, discouragement heavily weighting each syllable: "You're right. He's like all the others. We'll have to send him back."

"And look for no more?" The voice he recognized as Anthony faltered between question and statement.

A Babel of voices, in dispute; then, clearly, the voice Benson had come to label as Gregory, cut in:

"I will never give up!"

He raised his head; there was something in the timbre of that voice reminding him of his own feelings in the dark days when the UN had everywhere been reeling back under the Pan-Soviet hammer-blows.

"Anthony!" Gregory's voice again; Benson saw the speaker; short, stocky, grey-haired, stubborn lines about the mouth. The face of a man chasing an illusive but not uncapturable dream.

"That means nothing." A tall thin man, too lean for the tuniclike garment he wore, was shaking his head.

Deliberately, trying to remember his college courses in psychology, he forced himself to accept, and to assess, what he saw as reality. He was on a small table, like an operating table; the whole place looked like a medical lab or a clinic. He was still in uniform; his boots had soiled the white sheets with the dust of Armenia. He had all his equipment, including his pistol and combat-knife; his carbine was gone, however. He could feel the weight of his helmet on his head. The room still rocked and swayed a little, but the faces of the people were coming into focus.

He counted them, saying each number to himself: one, two, three, four, five men; one woman. He swung his feet over the edge of the table, being careful that it would be between him and the others when he rose, and began inching his right hand toward his right hip, using his left hand, on his brow, to misdirect attention.

"I would classify his actions as arising from conscious effort at cortico-thalamic integration," the woman said, like an archaeologist who has just found a K-ration tin at the bottom of a neolithic kitchen-midden. She had the peculiarly young-old look of the spinster teachers with whom Benson had worked before going to the war.

"I want to believe it, but I'm afraid to," another man for whom Benson had no name-association said. He was portly, grey-haired, arrogant-faced; he wore a short black jacket with a jeweled zipper-pull, and striped trousers.

Benson cleared his throat. "Just who are you people?" he inquired. "And just where am I?"

Anthony grabbed Gregory's hand and pumped it frantically.

"I've dreamed of the day when I could say this!" he cried. "Congratulations, Gregory!"

That touched off another bedlam, of joy, this time, instead of despair. Benson hid his amusement at the facility with which all of them were discovering in one another the courage, vision and stamina of true patriots and pioneers. He let it go on for a few moments, hoping to glean some clue. Finally, he interrupted.

"I believe I asked a couple of questions," he said, using the voice he reserved for sergeants and second lieutenants. "I hate to break up this mutual admiration session, but I would appreciate some answers. This isn't anything like the situation I last remember. . . ."

"He remembers!" Gregory exclaimed. "That confirms your first derivation by symbolic logic, and it strengthens the validity of the second. . . ."

The schoolteacherish woman began jabbering excitedly; she ran through about a paragraph of what was pure gobbledygook to Benson, before the man with the arrogant face and the jeweled zipper-pull broke in on her.

"Save that for later, Paula," he barked. "I'd be very much interested in your theories about why memories are unimpaired when you time-jump forward and lost when you reverse the process, but let's stick to business. We have what we wanted; now let's use what we have."

"I never liked the way you made your money," a dark-faced, cadaverous man said, "but when you talk, it makes sense. Let's get on with it."

Benson used the brief silence which followed to study the six. With the exception of the two who had just spoken, there was the indefinable mark of the fanatic upon all of them – people fanatical about different things, united for different reasons in a single purpose. It reminded him sharply of some teachers' committee about to beard a school-board with an unpopular and expensive recommendation.

Anthony – the oldest of the lot, in a knee-length tunic – turned to Gregory.

"I believe you had better. . . ." he began.

"As to who we are, we'll explain that, partially, later. As for your question, 'Where am I?' that will have to be rephrased. If you ask, 'When and where am I?' I can furnish a rational answer. In the temporal dimension, you are fifty years futureward of the day of your death; spatially, you are about eight thousand miles from the place of your death, in what is now the World Capitol, St. Louis."

Nothing in the answer made sense but the name of the city. Benson chuckled.

"What happened; the Cardinals conquer the world? I knew they had a good team, but I didn't think it was that good."

"No, no," Gregory told him earnestly. "The government isn't a theocracy. At least not yet. But if The Guide keeps on insisting that only beautiful things are good and that he is uniquely qualified to define beauty, watch his rule change into just that."

"I've been detecting symptoms of religious paranoia, messianic delusions, about his public statements. . . ." the woman began.

"Idolatry!" another member of the group, who wore a black coat fastened to the neck, and white neck-bands, rasped. "Idolatry in deed, as well as in spirit!"

The sense of unreality, partially dispelled, began to return. Benson dropped to the floor and stood beside the table, getting a cigarette out of his pocket and lighting it.

"I made a joke," he said, putting his lighter away. "The fact that none of you got it has done more to prove that I am fifty years in the future than anything any of you could say." He went on to explain who the St. Louis Cardinals were.

"Yes; I remember! Baseball!" Anthony exclaimed. "There is no baseball, now. The Guide will not allow competitive sports; he says that they foster the spirit of violence. . . ."

The cadaverous man in the blue jacket turned to the man in the black garment of similar cut.

"You probably know more history than any of us," he said, getting a cigar out of his pocket and lighting it. He lighted it by rubbing the end on the sole of his shoe. "Suppose you tell him what the score is." He turned to Benson. "You can rely on his dates and happenings; his interpretation's strictly capitalist, of course," he said.

Black-jacket shook his head. "You first, Gregory," he said. "Tell him how he got here, and then I'll tell him why."

"I believe," Gregory began, "that in your period, fiction writers made some use of the subject of time-travel. It was not, however, given serious consideration, largely because of certain alleged paradoxes involved, and because of an elementalistic and objectifying attitude toward the whole subject of time. I won't go into the mathematics and symbolic logic involved, but we have disposed of the objections; more, we have succeeded in constructing a time-machine, if you want to call it that. We prefer to call it a temporal-spatial displacement field generator."

"It's really very simple," the woman called Paula interrupted. "If the universe is expanding, time is a widening spiral; if contracting, a diminishing spiral; if static, a uniform spiral. The possibility of pulsation was our only worry. . . ."

"That's no worry," Gregory reproved her. "I showed you that the rate was too slow to have an effect on. . . ."

"Oh, nonsense; you can measure something which exists within a microsecond, but where is the instrument to measure a temporal pulsation that may require years. . .? You haven't come to that yet."

"Be quiet, both of you!" the man with the black coat and the white bands commanded. "While you argue about vanities, thousands are being converted to the godlessness of The Guide, and other thousands of his dupes are dying, unprepared to face their Maker!"

"All right, you invented a time-machine," Benson said. "In civvies, I was only a high school chemistry teacher. I can tell a class of juniors the difference between H_2O and H_2SO_4, but the theory of time-travel is wasted on me. . . . Suppose you just let me ask the questions; then I'll be sure of finding out what I don't know. For instance, who won the war I was fighting in, before you grabbed me and brought me here? The Commies?"

"No, the United Nations," Anthony told him. "At least, they were the least exhausted when both sides decided to quit."

"Then what's this dictatorship. . . . The Guide? Extreme Rightist?"

"Walter, you'd better tell him," Gregory said.

"We damn near lost the war," the man in the black jacket and striped trousers said, "but for once, we won the peace. The Soviet Bloc was broken up – India, China, Indonesia, Mongolia, Russia, the Ukraine, all the Satellite States. Most of them turned into little dictatorships, like the Latin American countries after the liberation from Spain, but they were personal, non-ideological, generally benevolent, dictatorships, the kind that can grow into democracies, if they're given time."

"Capitalistic dictatorships, he means," the cadaverous man in the blue jacket explained.

"Be quiet, Carl," Anthony told him. "Let's not confuse this with any class-struggle stuff."

"Actually, the United Nations rules the world," Walter continued. "What goes on in the Ukraine or Latvia or Manchuria is about analogous to what went on under the old United States government in, let's say, Tammany-ruled New York. But here's the catch. The UN is ruled absolutely by one man."

"How could that happen? In my time, the UN had its functions so subdivided and compartmented that it couldn't even run a war properly. Our army commanders were making war by systematic disobedience."

"The charter was changed shortly after . . . er, that is, after. . . ." Walter was fumbling for words.

"After my death." Benson finished politely. "Go on. Even with a changed charter, how did one man get all the powers into his hands?"

"By sorcery!" black-coat-and-white-bands fairly shouted. "By the help of his master, Satan!"

"You know, there are times when some such theory tempts me," Paula said.

"He was a big moneybags," Carl said. "He bribed his way in. See, New York was bombed flat. Where the old UN buildings were, it's still hot. So The Guide donated a big tract of land outside St. Louis, built these buildings – we're in the basement of one of them, right now, if you want a good laugh – and before long, he had the whole organization eating out of his hand. They just voted him into power, and the world into slavery."

Benson looked around at the others, who were nodding in varying degrees of agreement.

"Substantially, that's it. He managed to convince everybody of his altruism, integrity and wisdom," Walter said. "It was almost blasphemous to say anything against him. I really don't understand how it happened. . . ."

"Well, what's he been doing with his power?" Benson asked. "Wise things, or stupid ones?"

"I could be general, and say that he has deprived all of us of our political and other liberties. It is best to be specific," Anthony said. "Gregory?"

"My own field – dimensional physics – hasn't been interfered with much, yet. It's different in other fields. For instance, all research in sonics has been arbitrarily stopped. So has a great deal of work in organic and synthetic chemistry. Psychology is a madhouse of . . . what was the old word, licentiousness? No, lysenkoism. Medicine and surgery – well, there's a huge program of compulsory sterilization, and another one of eugenic marriage-control. And infants who don't conform to certain physical standards don't survive. Neither do people who have disfiguring accidents beyond the power of plastic surgery."

Paula spoke next. "My field is child welfare. Well, I'm going to show you an audio-visual of an interesting ceremony in a Hindu village, derived from the ancient custom of the suttee. It is the Hindu method of conforming to The Guide's demand that only beautiful children be allowed to grow to maturity."

The film was mercifully brief. Even in spite of the drums and gongs, and the chanting of the crowd, Benson found out how loudly a newborn infant can scream in a fire. The others looked as though they were going to be sick; he doubted if he looked much better.

"Of course, we are a more practical and mechanical-minded people, here and in Europe," Paula added, holding down her gorge by main strength. "We have lethal-gas chambers that even Hitler would have envied."

"I am a musician," Anthony said. "A composer. If Gregory thinks that the sciences are controlled, he should try to write even the simplest piece of music. The extent of censorship and control over all the arts, and especially music, is incredible." He coughed slightly. "And I have another motive, a more selfish one. I am approaching the compulsory retirement age; I will soon be invited to go to one of the Havens. Even though these Havens are located in the most barren places, they are beauty-spots, verdant beyond belief. It is of only passing interest that, while large numbers of the aged go there yearly, their populations remain constant, and, to judge from the quantities of supplies shipped to them, extremely small."

"They call me Samuel, in this organization," the man in the long black coat said. "Whoever gave me that alias must have chosen it because I am here in an effort to live up to it. Although I am ordained by no church, I fight for all of them. The plain fact is that this man we call The Guide is really the Antichrist!"

"Well, I haven't quite so lofty a motive, but it's good enough to make me willing to finance this project," Walter said. "It's very simple. The Guide won't let people make money, and if they do, he taxes it away from them. And he has laws to prohibit inheritance; what little you can accumulate, you can't pass on to your children."

"I put up a lot of the money, too, don't forget," Carl told him. "Or the Union did; I'm a poor man, myself." He was smoking an excellent cigar, for a poor man, and his clothes could have come from the same tailor as Walter's. "Look, we got a real Union – the Union of all unions. Every working man in North America, Europe, Australia and South Africa belongs to it. And The Guide has us all hog-tied."

"He won't let you strike," Benson chuckled.

"That's right. And what can we do? Why, we can't even make our closed-shop contracts stick. And as far as getting anything like a pay-raise. . . ."

"Good thing. Another pay-raise in some of my companies would bankrupt them, the way The Guide has us under his thumb. . . ." Walter began, but he was cut off.

"Well! It seems as though this Guide has done some good, if he's made you two realize that you're both on the same side, and that what hurts one hurts both," Benson said. "When I shipped out for Turkey in '77, neither Labor nor Management had learned that." He looked from one to another of them. "The Guide must have a really good bodyguard, with all the enemies he's made."

Gregory shook his head. "He lives virtually alone, in a very small house on the UN Capitol grounds. In fact, except for a small police-force, armed only with non-lethal stun-guns, your profession of arms is non-existent."

"I've been guessing what you want me to do," Benson said. "You want this Guide bumped off. But why can't any of you do it? Or, if it's too risky, at least somebody from your own time? Why me?"

"We can't. Everybody in the world today is conditioned against violence, especially the taking of human life," Anthony told him.

"Now, wait a moment!" This time, he was using the voice he would have employed in chiding a couple of Anatolian peasant partisans who were field-stripping a machine gun the wrong way. "Those babies in that film you showed me weren't dying of old age. . . ."

"That is not violence," Paula said bitterly. "That is humane beneficence. Ugly people would be unhappy, and would make others unhappy, in a world where everybody else is beautiful."

"And all these oppressive and tyrannical laws," Benson continued. "How does he enforce them, without violence, actual or threatened?"

Samuel started to say something about the Power of the Evil One; Paula, ignoring him, said:

"I really don't know; he just does it. Mass hypnotism of some sort. I know music has something to do with it, because there is always music, everywhere. This laboratory, for instance, was secretly soundproofed; we couldn't have worked here, otherwise."

"All right. I can see that you'd need somebody from the past, preferably a soldier, whose conditioning has been in favor rather than against violence. I'm not the only one you snatched, I take it?"

"No. We've been using that machine to pick up men from battlefields all over the world and all over history," Gregory said. "Until now, none of them could adjust. . . . Uggh!" He shuddered, looking even sicker than when the film was being shown.

"He's thinking," Walter said, "about a French officer from Waterloo who blew out his brains with a pocket-pistol on that table, and an English archer from Agincourt who ran amok with a dagger in here, and a trooper of the Seventh Cavalry from the Custer Massacre."

Gregory managed to overcome his revulsion. "You see, we were forced to take our subjects largely at random with regard to individual characteristics, mental attitudes, adaptability, et cetera." As long as he stuck to high order abstractions, he could control himself. "Aside from their professional lack of repugnance for violence, we took soldiers from battlefields because we could select men facing immediate death, whose removal from the past would not have any effect upon the casual chain of events affecting the present."

A warning buzzer rasped in Benson's brain. He nodded, poker-faced.

"I can see that," he agreed. "You wouldn't dare do anything to change the past. That was always one of the favorite paradoxes in time-travel fiction. . . . Well, I think I have the general picture. You have a dictator who is tyrannizing you; you want to get rid of him; you can't kill him yourselves. I'm opposed to dictators, myself; that – and the Selective Service law, of course – was why I was a soldier. I have no moral or psychological taboos against killing dictators, or anybody else. Suppose I cooperate with you; what's in it for me?"

There was a long silence. Walter and Carl looked at one another inquiringly; the others dithered helplessly. It was Carl who answered.

"Your return to your own time and place."

"And if I don't cooperate with you?"

"Guess when and where else we could send you," Walter said.

Benson dropped his cigarette and tramped it.

"Exactly the same time and place?" he asked.

"Well, the structure of space-time demands. . . ." Paula began.

"The spatio-temporal displacement field is capable of identifying that spot –" Gregory pointed to a ten-foot circle in front of a bank of sleek-cabineted, dial-studded machines "– with any set of space-time coordinates in the universe. However, to avoid disruption of the structure of space-time, we must return you to approximately the same point in space-time."

Benson nodded again, this time at the confirmation of his earlier suspicion. Well, while he was alive, he still had a chance.

"All right; tell me exactly what you want me to do."

A third outbreak of bedlam, this time of relief and frantic explanation.

"Shut up, all of you!" For so thin a man, Carl had an astonishing voice. "I worked this out, so let me tell it." He turned to Benson. "Maybe I'm tougher than the rest of them, or maybe I'm not as deeply conditioned. For one thing, I'm tone-deaf. Well, here's the way it is. Gregory can set the machine to function automatically. You stand where he shows you, press the button he shows you, and fifteen seconds later it'll take you forward in time five seconds and about a kilometer in space, to The Guide's office. He'll be at his desk now. You'll have forty-five seconds to do the job, from the time the field collapses around you till it rebuilds. Then you'll be taken back to your own time again. The whole thing's automatic."

"Can do," Benson agreed. "How do I kill him?"

"I'm getting sick!" Paula murmured weakly. Her face was whiter than her gown.

"Take care of her, Samuel. Both of you'd better get out of here," Gregory said.

"The Lord of Hosts is my strength, He will. . . . Uggggh!" Samuel gasped.

"Conditioning's getting him, too; we gotta be quick," Carl said. "Here. This is what you'll use." He handed Benson a two-inch globe of black plastic. "Take the damn thing, quick! Little button on the side; press it, and get it out of your hand fast. . . ." He retched. "Limited-effect bomb; everything within two-meter circle burned to nothing; outside that, great but not unendurable heat. Shut your eyes when you throw it. Flash almost blinding." He dropped his cigar and turned almost green in the face. Walter had a drink poured and handed it to him. "Uggh! Thanks, Walter." He downed it.

"Peculiar sort of thing for a non-violent people to manufacture," Benson said, looking at the bomb and then putting it in his jacket pocket.

"It isn't a weapon. Industrial; we use it in mining. I used plenty of them, in Walter's iron mines."

He nodded again. "Where do I stand, now?" he asked.

"Right over here." Gregory placed him in front of a small panel with three buttons. "Press the middle one, and step back into the small red circle and stand perfectly still while the field builds up and collapses. Face that way."

Benson drew his pistol and checked it; magazine full, a round in the chamber, safety on.

"Put that horrid thing out of sight!" Anthony gasped. "The . . . the other thing . . . is what you want to use."

"The bomb won't be any good if some of his guards come in before the field re-builds," Benson said.

"He has no guards. He lives absolutely alone. We told you. . . ."

"I know you did. You probably believed it, too. I don't. And by the way, you're sending me forward. What do you do about the fact that a time-jump seems to make me pass out?"

"Here. Before you press the button, swallow it." Gregory gave him a small blue pill.

"Well, I guess that's all there is," Gregory continued. "I hope. . . ." His face twitched, and he dropped to the floor with a thud. Carl and Walter came forward, dragged him away from the machine.

"Conditioning got him. Getting me, too," Walter said. "Hurry up, man!"

Benson swallowed the pill, pressed the button and stepped back into the red circle, drawing his pistol and snapping off the safety. The blue mist closed in on him.

This time, however, it did not thicken into blackness. It became luminous, brightening to a dazzle and dimming again to a colored mist, and then it cleared, while Benson stood at raise pistol, as though on a target range. He was facing a big desk at twenty feet, across a thick-piled blue rug. There was a man seated at the desk, a white-haired man with a mustache and a small beard, who wore a loose coat of some glossy plum-brown fabric, and a vividly blue neck-scarf.

The pistol centered on the v-shaped blue under his chin. Deliberately, Benson squeezed, recovered from the recoil, aimed, fired, recovered, aimed, fired. Five seconds gone. The old man slumped across the desk, his arms extended. Better make a good job of it, six, seven, eight seconds; he stepped forward to the edge of the desk, call that fifteen seconds, and put the muzzle to the top of the man's head, firing again and snapping on the safety. There had been something familiar about The Guide's face, but it was too late to check on that, now. There wasn't any face left; not even much head.

A box, on the desk, caught Benson's eye, a cardboard box with an envelope, stamped *Top Secret! For the Guide Only!* taped to it. He holstered his pistol and caught that up, stuffing it into his pocket, in obedience to an instinct to grab anything that looked like intelligence matter while in the enemy's country. Then he stepped back to the spot where the field had deposited him. He had ten seconds to spare; somebody was banging on a door when the blue mist began to gather around him.

He was crouching, the spherical plastic object in his right hand, his thumb over the button, when the field collapsed. Sure enough, right in front of him, so close that he could smell the very heat of it, was the big tank with the red star on its turret. He cursed the sextet of sanctimonious double-crossers eight thousand miles and fifty years away in space-time. The machine guns had stopped – probably because they couldn't be depressed far enough to aim at him, now; that was a notorious fault of some of the newer Pan-Soviet tanks – and he rocked back on his heels, pressed the button, and heaved, closing his eyes. As the thing left his fingers, he knew that he had thrown too hard. His muscles, accustomed to the heavier cast-iron grenades of his experience, had betrayed him. For a moment, he was closer to despair than at any other time in the whole phantasmagoric adventure. Then he was hit, with physical violence, by a wave of almost solid heat. It didn't smell like the heat of the tank's engines; it smelled like molten metal, with undertones of burned flesh. Immediately, there was a multiple explosion that threw him flat, as the tank's ammunition went up. There were no screams. It was too fast for that. He opened his eyes.

The turret and top armor of the tank had vanished. The two massive treads had been toppled over, one to either side. The body had collapsed between them, and it was running sticky trickles of molten metal. He blinked, rubbed his eyes on the back of his hand, and looked again. Of all the many blasted and burned-out tanks, Soviet and UN, that he had seen, this was the most completely wrecked thing in his experience. And he'd done that with one grenade. . . .

At that moment, there was a sudden rushing overhead, and an instant later the barrage began falling beyond the crest of the ridge. He looked at his watch, blinked, and looked again. That barrage was due at 0550; according to the watch, it was 0726. He was sure that, ten minutes ago, when he had looked at it, up there at the head of the ravine, it had been twenty minutes to six. He puzzled about that for a moment, and decided that he must have caught the stem on something and pulled it out, and then twisted it a little, setting the watch ahead. Then, somehow, the stem had gotten pushed back in, starting it at the new setting. That was a pretty far-fetched explanation, but it was the only one he could think of.

But about this tank, now. He was positive that he could remember throwing a grenade. . . . Yet he'd used his last grenade back there at the supply dump. He saw his carbine, and picked it up. That silly blackout he'd had, for a second, there; he must have dropped it. Action was open, empty magazine on the ground where he'd dropped it. He wondered, stupidly, if one of his bullets couldn't have gone down the muzzle of the tank's gun and exploded the shell in the chamber. . . . Oh, the hell with it! The tank might have been hit by a premature shot from the barrage which was raging against the far slope of the ridge. He reset his watch by guess and looked down the valley. The big attack would be starting any minute, now, and there would be fleeing Commies coming up the valley ahead of the UN advance. He'd better get himself placed before they started coming in on him.

He stopped thinking about the mystery of the blown-up tank, a solution to which seemed to dance maddeningly just out of his mental reach, and found himself a place among the rocks to wait. Down the valley he could hear everything from pistols to mortars going off, and shouting in three or four racial intonations. After a while, fugitive Communists began coming, many of them without their equipment, stumbling in their haste and looking back over their shoulders. Most of them avoided the mouth of the ravine and hurried by to the left or right, but one little clump, eight or ten, came up the dry stream-bed, and stopped a hundred and fifty yards from his hiding place to make a stand. They were Hindus, with outsize helmets over their turbans. Two of them came ahead, carrying a machine gun, followed by a third with a flame-thrower; the others retreated more slowly, firing their rifles to delay pursuit.

Cuddling the stock of his carbine to his cheek, he divided a ten-shot burst between the two machine-gunners, then, as a matter of principle, he shot the man with the flame-thrower. He had a dislike for flame-throwers; he killed every enemy he found with one. The others dropped their rifles and raised their hands, screaming: "Hey, Joe! Hey, Joe! You no shoot, me no shoot!"

A dozen men in UN battledress came up and took them prisoner. Benson shouted to them, and then rose and came down to join them. They were British – Argyle and Sutherland Highlanders, advertising the fact by inconspicuous bits of tartan on their uniforms. The subaltern in command looked at him and nodded.

"Captain Benson? We were warned to be on watch for your patrol," he said. "Any of the rest of you lads get out?"

Benson shrugged. "We split up after the attack. You may run into a couple of them. Some are locals and don't speak very good English. I've got to get back to Division, myself; what's the best way?"

"Down that way. You'll overtake a couple of our walking wounded. If you don't mind going slowly, they'll show you the way to advance dressing station, and you can hitch a ride on an ambulance from there."

Benson nodded. Off on the left, there was a flurry of small-arms fire, ending in yells of "Hey, Joe! Hey, Joe!" – the World War IV version of "Kamarad!"

His company was a non-T/O outfit; he came directly under Division command and didn't have to bother reporting to any regimental or brigade commanders. He walked for an hour with half a dozen lightly wounded Scots, rode for another hour on a big cat-truck loaded with casualties of six regiments and four races, and finally reached Division Rear, where both the Division and Corps commanders took time to compliment him on the part his last hunter patrol had played in the now complete breakthrough. His replacement, an equine-faced Spaniard with an imposing display of fruit-salad, was there, too; he solemnly took off the bracelet a refugee Caucasian goldsmith had made for his predecessor's predecessor and gave it to the new commander of what had formerly been Benson's Butchers. As he had expected, there was also another medal waiting for him.

A medical check at Task Force Center got him a warning; his last patrol had brought him dangerously close to the edge of combat fatigue. Remembering the incidents of the tank and the unaccountably fast watch, and the mysterious box and envelope which he had found in his coat pocket, he agreed, saying nothing about the questions that were puzzling him. The Psychological Department was never too busy to refuse another case; they hunted patients gleefully, each psych-shark seeking in every one proof of his own particular theories. It was with relief that he watched them fill out the red tag which gave him a priority on jet transports for home.

Ankara to Alexandria, Alexandria to Dakar, Dakar to Belém, Belém to the shattered skyline of New York, the "hurry-and-wait" procedures at Fort Carlisle, and, after the usual separation promotion, Major Fred Benson, late of Benson's Butchers, was back at teaching high school juniors the difference between H_2O and H_2SO_4.

There were two high schools in the city: McKinley High, on the east side, and Dwight Eisenhower High, on the west. A few blocks from McKinley was the Tulip Tavern, where the Eisenhower teachers came in the late afternoons; the McKinley faculty crossed town to do their after-school drinking on the west side. When Benson entered the Tulip Tavern, on a warm September afternoon, he found Bill Myers, the school psychologist, at one of the tables, smoking his pipe, checking over a stack of aptitude test forms, and drinking beer. He got a highball at the bar and carried it over to Bill's table.

"Oh, hi, Fred." The psychologist separated the finished from the unfinished work with a sheet of yellow paper and crammed the whole business into his brief case. "I was hoping somebody'd show up. . . ."

Benson lit a cigarette, sipped his highball. They talked at random – school-talk; the progress of the war, now in its twelfth year; personal reminiscences, of the Turkish Theater where Benson had served, and the Madras Beachhead, where Myers had been.

"Bring home any souvenirs?" Myers asked.

"Not much. Couple of pistols, couple of knives, some pictures. I don't remember what all; haven't gotten around to unpacking them, yet. . . . I have a sixth of rye and some beer, at my rooms. Let's go around and see what I did bring home."

They finished their drinks and went out.

"What the devil's that?" Myers said, pointing to the cardboard box with the envelope taped to it, when Benson lifted it out of the grey-green locker.

"Bill, I don't know," Benson said. "I found it in the pocket of my coat, on my way back from my last hunter patrol. . . . I've never told anybody about this, before."

"That's the damnedest story I've ever heard, and in my racket you hear some honeys," Myers said, when he had finished. "You couldn't have picked that thing up in some other way, deliberately forgotten the circumstances, and fabricated this story about the tank and the grenade and the discrepancy in your watch subconsciously as an explanation?"

"My subconscious is a better liar than that," Benson replied. "It would have cobbled up some kind of a story that would stand up. This business. . . ."

"Top Secret! For the Guide Only!" Myers frowned. "That isn't one of our marks, and if it were Soviet, it'd be tri-lingual, Russian, Hindi and Chinese."

"Well, let's see what's in it. I want this thing cleared up. I've been having some of the nastiest dreams, lately. . . ."

"Well, be careful; it may be booby-trapped," Myers said urgently.

"Don't worry; I will."

He used a knife to slice the envelope open without untaping it from the box, and exposed five sheets of typewritten onion-skin paper. There was no letterhead, no salutation or address-line. Just a mass of chemical formulae, and a concise report on tests. It seemed to be a report on an improved syrup for a carbonated soft-drink. There were a few cryptic cautionary references to heightened physico-psychological effects.

The box was opened with the same caution, but it proved as innocent of dangers as the envelope. It contained only a half-liter bottle, wax-sealed, containing a dark reddish-brown syrup.

"There's a lot of this stuff I don't dig," Benson said, tapping the sheets of onion-skin. "I don't even scratch the surface of this rigmarole about The Guide. I'm going to get to work on this sample in the lab, at school, though. Maybe we have something, here."

At eight-thirty the next evening, after four and a half hours work, he stopped to check what he had found out.

The school's X-ray, an excellent one, had given him a complete picture of the molecular structure of the syrup. There were a couple of long-chain molecules that he could only believe after two re-examinations and a careful check of the machine, but with the help of the notes he could deduce how they had been put together. They would be the Ingredient Alpha and Ingredient Beta referred to in the notes.

The components of the syrup were all simple and easily procurable with these two exceptions, as were the basic components from which these were made.

The mechanical guinea-pig demonstrated that the syrup contained nothing harmful to human tissue.

Of course, there were the warnings about heightened psychophysiological effects. . . .

He stuck a poison-label on the bottle, locked it up, and went home. The next day, he and Bill Myers got a bottle of carbonated water and mixed themselves a couple of drinks of it. It was delicious – sweet, dry, tart, sour, all of these in alternating waves of pleasure.

"We do have something, Bill," he said. "We have something that's going to give our income-tax experts headaches."

"You have," Myers corrected. "Where do you start fitting me into it?"

"We're a good team, Bill. I'm a chemist, but I don't know a thing about people. You're a psychologist. A real one; not one of these night-school boys. A juvenile psychologist, too. And what age-group spends the most money in this country for soft-drinks?"

Knowing the names of the syrup's ingredients, and what their molecular structure was like, was only the beginning. Gallon after gallon of the School Board's chemicals went down the laboratory sink; Fred Benson and Bill Myers almost lived in the fourth floor lab. Once or twice there were head-shaking warnings from the principal about the dangers of overwork. The watchmen, at all hours, would hear the occasional twanging of Benson's guitar in the laboratory, and know that he had come to a dead end on something and was trying to think. Football season came and went; basketball season; the inevitable riot between McKinley and Eisenhower rooters; the Spring concerts. The term-end exams were only a month away when Benson and Myers finally did it, and stood solemnly, each with a beaker in either hand and took alternate sips of the original and the drink mixed from the syrup they had made.

"Not a bit of difference, Fred," Myers said. "We have it!"

Benson picked up the guitar and began plunking on it.

"Hey!" Myers exclaimed. "Have you been finding time to take lessons on that thing? I never heard you play as well as that!"

They decided to go into business in St. Louis. It was centrally located, and, being behind more concentric circles of radar and counter-rocket defenses, it was in better shape than any other city in the country and most likely to stay that way. Getting started wasn't hard; the first banker who tasted the new drink-named Evri-Flave, at Myers' suggestion – couldn't dig up the necessary money fast enough. Evri-Flave hit the market with a bang and became an instant success; soon the rainbow-tinted vending machines were everywhere, dispensing the slender, slightly flattened bottles and devouring quarters voraciously. In spite of high taxes and the difficulties of doing business in a consumers' economy upon which a war-time economy had been superimposed, both Myers and Benson were rapidly becoming wealthy. The gregarious Myers installed himself in a luxurious apartment in the city; Benson bought a large tract of land down the river toward Carondelet and started building a home and landscaping the grounds.

The dreams began bothering him again, now that the urgency of getting Evri-Flave, Inc., started had eased. They were not dreams of the men he had killed in battle, or, except for one about a huge, hot-smelling tank with a red star on the turret, about the war. Generally, they were about a strange, beautiful, office-room, in which a young man in uniform killed an older man in a plum-brown coat and a vivid blue neck-scarf. Sometimes Benson identified himself with the killer; sometimes with the old man who was killed.

He talked to Myers about these dreams, but beyond generalities about delayed effects of combat fatigue and vague advice to relax, the psychologist, now head of Sales & Promotion of Evri-Flave, Inc., could give him no help.

The war ended three years after the new company was launched. There was a momentary faltering of the economy, and then the work of reconstruction was crying hungrily for all the labor and capital that had been idled by the end of destruction, and more. There was a new flood-tide of prosperity, and Evri-Flave rode the crest. The estate at Carondelet was finished – a beautiful place, surrounded with gardens, fragrant with flowers, full of the songs of birds and soft music from concealed record-players. It made him forget the ugliness of the war, and kept the dreams from returning so frequently. All the world ought to be like that, he thought; beautiful and quiet and peaceful. People surrounded with such beauty couldn't think about war.

All the world could be like that, if only. . . .

The UN chose St. Louis for its new headquarters – many of its offices had been moved there after the second and most destructive bombing of New York – and when the city by the Mississippi began growing into a real World Capital, the flow of money into it almost squared overnight. Benson began to take an active part in politics in the new World Sovereignty party. He did not, however, allow his political activities to distract him from the work of expanding the company to which he owed his wealth and position. There were always things to worry about.

"I don't know," Myers said to him, one evening, as they sat over a bottle of rye in the psychologist's apartment. "I could make almost as much money practicing as a psychiatrist, these days. The whole world seems to be going pure, unadulterated nuts! That affair in Munich, for instance."

"Yes." Benson grimaced as he thought of the affair in Munich – a Wagnerian concert which had terminated in an insane orgy of mass suicide. "Just a week after we started our free-sample campaign in South Germany, too. . . ."

He stopped short, downing his drink and coughing over it.

"Bill! You remember those sheets of onion-skin in that envelope?"

"The foundation of our fortunes; I wonder where you really did get that. . . . Fred!" His eyes widened in horror. "That caution about 'heightened psychophysiological effects,' that we were never able to understand!"

Benson nodded grimly. "And think of all the crazy cases of mass-hysteria – that baseball-game riot in Baltimore; the time everybody started tearing off each others' clothes in Milwaukee; the sex-orgy in New Orleans. And the sharp uptrend in individual psychoneurotic and psychotic behavior. All in connection with music, too, and all after Evri-Flave got on the market."

"We'll have to stop it; pull Evri-Flave off the market," Myers said. "We can't be responsible for letting this go on."

"We can't stop, either. There's at least a two months' supply out in the hands of jobbers and distributors over whom we have no control. And we have all these contractual obligations, to buy the entire output of the companies that make the syrup for us; if we stop buying, they can sell it in competition with us, as long as they don't infringe our trade-name. And we can't prevent pirating. You know how easily we were able to duplicate that sample I brought back from Turkey. Why, our legal department's kept busy all the time prosecuting unlicensed manufacturers as it is."

"We've got to do something, Fred!" There was almost a whiff of hysteria in Myers' voice.

"We will. We'll start, first thing tomorrow, on a series of tests – just you and I, like the old times at Eisenhower High. First, we want to be sure that Evri-Flave really is responsible. It'd be a hell of a thing if we started a public panic against our own product for nothing. And then. . . ."

It took just two weeks, in a soundproofed and guarded laboratory on Benson's Carondelet estate, to convict their delicious drink of responsibility for that Munich State Opera House Horror and everything else. Reports from confidential investigators in Munich confirmed this. It had, of course, been impossible to interview the two thousand men and women who had turned the Opera House into a pyre for their own immolation, but none of the tiny minority who had kept their sanity and saved their lives had tasted Evri-Flave.

It took another month to find out exactly how the stuff affected the human nervous system, and they almost wrecked their own nervous systems in the process. The real villain, they discovered, was the incredible-looking long-chain compound alluded to in the original notes as Ingredient Beta; its principal physiological effect was to greatly increase the sensitivity of the aural nerves. Not only was the hearing range widened – after consuming thirty CC of Beta, they could hear the sound of an ultrasonic dog-whistle quite plainly – but the very quality of all audible sounds was curiously enhanced and altered. Myers, the psychologist, who was also well grounded in neurology, explained how the chemical produced this effect; it meant about as much to Benson as some of his chemistry did to Bill Myers. There was also a secondary, purely psychological, effect. Certain musical chords had definite effects on the emotions of the hearer, and the subject, beside being directly influenced by the music, was rendered extremely open to verbal suggestions accompanied by a suitable musical background.

Benson transferred the final results of this stage of the research to the black notebook and burned the scratch-sheets.

"That's how it happened, then," he said. "The Munich thing was the result of all that Götterdämmerung music. There was a band at the baseball park in Baltimore. The New Orleans Orgy started while a local radio station was broadcasting some of this new dance-music. Look, these tone-clusters, here, have a definite sex-excitation effect. This series of six chords, which occur in some of the Wagnerian stuff; effect, a combined feeling of godlike isolation and despair. And these consecutive fifths – a sense of danger, anger, combativeness. You know, we could work out a whole range of emotional stimuli to fit the effects of Ingredient Beta. . . ."

"We don't want to," Myers said. "We want to work out a substitute for Beta that will keep the flavor of the drink without the psychophysiological effects."

"Yes, sure. I have some of the boys at the plant lab working on that. Gave them a lot of syrup without Beta, and told them to work out cheap additives to restore the regular Evri-Flave taste; told them it was an effort to find a cheap substitute for an expensive ingredient. But look, Bill. You and I both see, for instance, that a powerful world-wide supra-national sovereignty is the only guarantee of world peace. If we could use something like this to help overcome antiquated verbal prejudices and nationalistic emotional attachments. . . ."

"No!" Myers said. "I won't ever consent to anything like that, Fred! Not even in a cause like world peace; use a thing like this for a good, almost holy, cause now, and tomorrow we, or those who would come after us, would be using it to create a tyranny. You know what year this is, Bill?"

"Why, 1984," Benson said.

"Yes. You remember that old political novel of Orwell's, written about forty years ago? Well, that's a picture of the kind of world you'd have, eventually, no matter what kind of a world you started out to make. Fred, don't ever think of using this stuff for a purpose like that. If you try it, I'll fight you with every resource I have."

There was a fanatical, almost murderous, look in Bill Myers' eyes. Benson put the notebook in his pocket, then laughed and threw up his hands.

"Hey, Joe! Hey, Joe!" he cried. "You're right, of course, Bill. We can't even trust the UN with a thing like this. It makes the H-bomb look like a stone hatchet. . . . Well, I'll call Grant, at the plant lab, and see how his boys are coming along with the substitute; as soon as we get it, we can put out a confidential letter to all our distributors and syrup-manufacturers. . . ."

He walked alone in the garden at Carondelet, watching the color fade out of the sky and the twilight seep in among the clipped yews. All the world could be like this garden, a place of peace and beauty and quiet, if only. . . . All the world *would* be a beautiful and peaceful garden, in his own lifetime! He had the means of making it so!

Three weeks later, he murdered his friend and partner, Bill Myers. It was a suicide; nobody but Fred Benson knew that he had taken fifty CC of pure Ingredient Beta in a couple of cocktails while listening to the queer phonograph record that he had played half an hour before blowing his brains out.

The decision had cost Benson a battle with his conscience from which he had emerged the sole survivor. The conscience was buried along with Bill Myers, and all that remained was a purpose.

Evri-Flave stayed on the market unaltered. The night before the national election, the World Sovereignty party distributed thousands of gallons of Evri-Flave; their speakers, on every radio and television network, were backgrounded by soft music. The next day, when the vote was counted, it was found that the American Nationalists had carried a few backwoods precincts in the Rockies and the Southern Appalachians and one county in Alaska, where there had been no distribution of Evri-Flave.

The dreams came back more often, now that Bill Myers was gone. Benson was only beginning to realize what a large fact in his life the companionship of the young psychologist had been. Well, a world of peace and beauty was an omelet worth the breaking of many eggs. . . .

He purchased another great tract of land near the city, and donated it to the UN for their new headquarters buildings; the same architects and landscapists who had created the estate at Carondelet were put to work on it. In the middle of what was to become World City, they erected a small home for Fred Benson. Benson was often invited to address the delegates to the UN; always, there was soft piped-in music behind his words. He saw to it that Evri-Flave was available free to all UN personnel. The Senate of the United States elected him as perpetual U. S. delegate-in-chief to the UN; not long after, the Security Council elected him their perpetual chairman.

In keeping with his new dignities, and to ameliorate his youthful appearance, he grew a mustache and, eventually, a small beard. The black notebook in which he kept the records of his experiments was always with him; page after page was filled with notes. Experiments in sonics, like the one which had produced the ultrasonic stun-gun which rendered lethal weapons unnecessary for police and defense purposes, or the new musical combinations with which he was able to play upon every emotion and instinct.

But he still dreamed, the same recurring dream of the young soldier and the old man in the office. By now, he was consistently identifying himself with the latter. He took to carrying one of the thick-barreled stun-pistols always, now. Alone, he practiced constantly with it, drawing, breaking soap-bubbles with the concentrated sound-waves it projected. It was silly, perhaps, but it helped him in his dreams. Now, the old man with whom he identified himself would draw a stun-pistol, occasionally, to defend himself.

The years drained one by one through the hourglass of Time. Year after year, the world grew more peaceful, more beautiful. There were no more incidents like the mass-suicide of Munich or the mass-perversions of New Orleans; the playing and even the composing of music was strictly controlled – no dangerous notes or chords could be played in a world drenched with Ingredient Beta. Steadily the idea grew that peace and beauty were supremely good, that violence and ugliness were supremely evil. Even competitive sports which simulated violence; even children born ugly and misshapen. . . .

He finished the breakfast which he had prepared for himself – he trusted no food that another had touched – and knotted the vivid blue scarf about his neck before slipping into the loose coat of glossy plum-brown, then checked the stun-pistol and pocketed the black notebook, its plastileather cover glossy from long use. He stood in front of the mirror, brushing his beard, now snow-white. Two years, now, and he would be eighty – had he been anyone but The Guide, he would have long ago retired to the absolute peace and repose of one of the Elders' Havens. Peace and repose, however, were not for The Guide; it would take another twenty years to finish his task of remaking the world, and he would need every day of it that his medical staff could borrow or steal for him. He made an eye-baffling practice draw with the stun-pistol, then holstered it and started down the spiral stairway to the office below.

There was the usual mass of papers on his desk. A corps of secretaries had screened out everything but what required his own personal and immediate attention, but the business of guiding a world could only be reduced to a certain point. On top was the digest of the world's news for the past twenty-four hours, and below that was the agenda for the afternoon's meeting of the Council. He laid both in front of him, reading over the former and occasionally making a note on the latter. Once his glance strayed to the cardboard box in front of him, with the envelope taped to it – the latest improvement on the Evri-Flave syrup, with the report from his own chemists, all conditioned to obedience, loyalty and secrecy. If they thought he was going to try that damned stuff on himself. . . .

There was a sudden gleam of light in the middle of the room, in front of his desk. No, a mist, through which a blue light seemed to shine. The stun-pistol was in his hand – his instinctive reaction to anything unusual – and pointed into the shining mist when it vanished and a man appeared in front of him; a man in the baggy green combat-uniform that he himself had worn fifty years before; a man with a heavy automatic pistol in his hand. The gun was pointed directly at him.

The Guide aimed quickly and pressed the trigger of the ultrasonic stunner. The pistol dropped soundlessly on the thick-piled rug; the man in uniform slumped in an inert heap. The Guide sprang to his feet and rounded the desk, crossing to and bending over the intruder. Why, this was the dream that had plagued him through the years. But it was ending differently. The young man – his face was startlingly familiar, somehow – was not killing the old man. Those years of practice with the stun-pistol. . . .

He stooped and picked the automatic up. The young man was unconscious, and The Guide had his pistol, now. He slipped the automatic into his pocket and straightened beside his inert would-be slayer.

A shimmering globe of blue mist appeared around them, brightened to a dazzle, and dimmed again to a colored mist before it vanished, and when it cleared away, he was standing beside the man in uniform, in the sandy bed of a dry stream at the mouth of a little ravine, and directly in front of him, looming above him, was a thing that had not been seen in the world for close to half a century – a big, hot-smelling tank with a red star on its turret.

He might have screamed – the din of its treads and engines deafened him – and, in panic, he turned and ran, his old legs racing, his old heart pumping madly. The noise of the tank increased as machine guns joined the uproar. He felt the first bullet strike him, just above the hips – no pain; just a tremendous impact. He might have felt the second bullet, too, as the ground tilted and rushed up at his face. Then he was diving into a tunnel of blackness that had no end. . . .

Captain Fred Benson, of Benson's Butchers, had been jerked back into consciousness when the field began to build around him. He was struggling to rise, fumbling the grenade out of his pocket, when it collapsed. Sure enough, right in front of him, so close that he could smell the very heat of it, was the big tank with the red star on its turret. He cursed the sextet of sanctimonious double-crossers eight thousand miles and fifty years away in space-time. The machine guns had stopped – probably because they couldn't be depressed far enough to aim at him, now; that was a notorious fault of some of the newer Pan-Soviet tanks. He had the bomb out of his pocket, when the machine guns began firing again, this time at something on his left. Wondering what had created the diversion, he rocked back on his heels, pressed the button, and heaved, closing his eyes. As the thing left his fingers, he knew that he had thrown too hard. His muscles, accustomed to the heavier cast-iron grenades, had betrayed him. For a moment, he was closer to despair than at any other time in the whole phantasmagoric adventure. Then he was hit, with physical force, by a wave of almost solid heat. It didn't smell like the heat of the tank's engines; it smelled like molten metal, with undertones of burned flesh. Immediately, there was a multiple explosion that threw him flat, as the tank's ammunition went up. There were no screams. It was too fast for that. He opened his eyes.

The turret and top armor of the tank had vanished. The two massive treads had been toppled over, one to either side. The body had collapsed between them, and it was running sticky trickles of molten metal. He blinked, rubbed his eyes on the back of his hand, and looked again. Of all the many blasted and burned-out tanks, Soviet and UN, that he had seen, this was the most completely wrecked thing in his experience. And he'd done that with one grenade. . . .

Remembering the curious manner in which, at the last, the tank had begun firing at something to the side, he looked around, to see the crumpled body in the pale violet-grey trousers and the plum-brown coat. Finding his carbine and reloading it, he went over to the dead man, turning the body over. He was an old man, with a white mustache and a small white beard – why, if the mustache were smaller and there were no beard, he would pass for Benson's own father, who had died in 1962. The clothes weren't Turkish or Armenian or Persian, or anything one would expect in this country.

The old man had a pistol in his coat pocket, and Benson pulled it out and looked at it, then did a double-take and grabbed for his own holster, to find it empty. The pistol was his own 9.5 Colt automatic. He looked at the dead man, with the white beard and the vivid blue neck-scarf, and he was sure that he had never seen him before. He'd had that pistol when he'd come down the ravine. . . .

There was another pistol under the dead man's coat, in a shoulder-holster; a queer thing with a thick round barrel, like an old percussion pepper-box, and a diaphragm instead of a muzzle. Probably projected ultrasonic waves. He holstered his own Colt and pocketed the unknown weapon. There was a black plastileather-bound notebook. It was full of notes. Chemical formulae, yes, and some stuff on sonics; that tied in with the queer pistol. He pocketed that. He'd look both over, when he had time and privacy, two scarce commodities in the Army. . . .

At that moment, there was a sudden rushing overhead, and an instant later, the barrage began falling beyond the crest of the ridge. He looked at his watch, blinked, and looked again. That barrage was due at 0550; according to his watch, it was 0726. That was another mystery, to go with the question of who the dead man was, where he had come from, and how he'd gotten hold of Benson's pistol. Yes, and how that tank had gotten blown up. Benson was sure he had used his last grenade back at the supply-dump.

The hell with it; he'd worry about all that later. The attack was due any minute, now, and there would be fleeing Commies coming up the valley ahead, of the UN advance. He'd better get himself placed before they started coming in on him.

He stopped thinking about the multiple mystery, a solution to which seemed to dance maddeningly just out of his mental reach, and found himself a place among the rocks to wait, and while he waited, he looked over the plastileather-bound notebook. In civil life, he had been a high school chemistry teacher, but the stuff in this book was utterly new to him. Some of it he could understand readily enough; the rest of it he could dig out for himself. Stuff about some kind of a carbonated soft-drink, and about a couple of unbelievable-looking long-chain molecules. . . .

After a while, fugitive Communists began coming up the valley to make their stand.

Benson put away the notebook, picked up his carbine, and cuddled the stock to his cheek. . . .

The End

Dearest

Colonel Ashley Hampton chewed his cigar and forced himself to relax, his glance slowly traversing the room, lingering on the mosaic of book-spines in the tall cases, the sunlight splashed on the faded pastel colors of the carpet, the soft-tinted autumn landscape outside the French windows, the trophies of Indian and Filipino and German weapons on the walls. He could easily feign relaxation here in the library of "Greyrock," as long as he looked only at these familiar inanimate things and avoided the five people gathered in the room with him, for all of them were enemies.

There was his nephew, Stephen Hampton, greying at the temples but youthfully dressed in sports-clothes, leaning with obvious if slightly premature proprietorship against the fireplace, a whiskey-and-soda in his hand. There was Myra, Stephen's smart, sophisticated-looking blonde wife, reclining in a chair beside the desk. For these two, he felt an implacable hatred. The others were no less enemies, perhaps more dangerous enemies, but they were only the tools of Stephen and Myra. For instance, T. Barnwell Powell, prim and self-satisfied, sitting on the edge of his chair and clutching the briefcase on his lap as though it were a restless pet which might attempt to escape. He was an honest man, as lawyers went; painfully ethical. No doubt he had convinced himself that his clients were acting from the noblest and most disinterested motives. And Doctor Alexis Vehrner, with his Vandyke beard and his Viennese accent as phony as a Soviet-controlled election, who had preempted the chair at Colonel Hampton's desk. That rankled the old soldier, but Doctor Vehrner would want to assume the position which would give him appearance of commanding the situation, and he probably felt that Colonel Hampton was no longer the master of "Greyrock." The fifth, a Neanderthal type in a white jacket, was Doctor Vehrner's attendant and bodyguard; he could be ignored, like an enlisted man unthinkingly obeying the orders of a superior.

"But you are not cooperating, Colonel Hampton," the psychiatrist complained. "How can I help you if you do not cooperate?"

Colonel Hampton took the cigar from his mouth. His white mustache, tinged a faint yellow by habitual smoking, twitched angrily.

"Oh; you call it helping me, do you?" he asked acidly.

"But why else am I here?" the doctor parried.

"You're here because my loving nephew and his charming wife can't wait to see me buried in the family cemetery; they want to bury me alive in that private Bedlam of yours," Colonel Hampton replied.

"See!" Myra Hampton turned to the psychiatrist. "We are *persecuting* him! We are all *envious* of him! We are *plotting against* him!"

"Of course; this sullen and suspicious silence is a common paranoid symptom; one often finds such symptoms in cases of senile dementia," Doctor Vehrner agreed.

Colonel Hampton snorted contemptuously. Senile dementia! Well, he must have been senile and demented, to bring this pair of snakes into his home, because he felt an obligation to his dead brother's memory. And he'd willed "Greyrock," and his money, and everything, to Stephen. Only Myra couldn't wait till he died; she'd Lady-Macbethed her husband into this insanity accusation.

". . . however, I must fully satisfy myself, before I can sign the commitment," the psychiatrist was saying. "After all, the patient is a man of advanced age. Seventy-eight, to be exact."

Seventy-eight; almost eighty. Colonel Hampton could hardly realize that he had been around so long. He had been a little boy, playing soldiers. He had been a young man, breaking the family tradition of Harvard and wangling an appointment to West Point. He had been a new second lieutenant at a little post in Wyoming, in the last dying flicker of the Indian Wars. He had been a first lieutenant, trying to make soldiers of militiamen and hoping for orders to Cuba before the Spaniards gave up. He had been the hard-bitten captain of a hard-bitten company, fighting Moros in the jungles of Mindanao. Then, through the early years of the Twentieth Century, after his father's death, he had been that *rara avis* in the American service, a really wealthy professional officer. He had played polo, and served a turn as military attaché at the Paris embassy. He had commanded a regiment in France in 1918, and in the post-war years, had rounded out his service in command of a regiment of Negro cavalry, before retiring to "Greyrock." Too old for active service, or even a desk at the Pentagon, he had drilled a Home Guard company of 4-Fs and boys and paunchy middle-agers through the Second World War. Then he had been an old man, sitting alone in the sunlight . . . until a wonderful thing had happened.

"Get him to tell you about this invisible playmate of his," Stephen suggested. "If that won't satisfy you, I don't know what will."

It had begun a year ago last June. He had been sitting on a bench on the east lawn, watching a kitten playing with a crumpled bit of paper on the walk, circling warily around it as though it were some living prey, stalking cautiously, pouncing and striking the paper ball with a paw and then pursuing it madly. The kitten, whose name was Smokeball, was a friend of his; soon she would tire of her game and jump up beside him to be petted.

Then suddenly, he seemed to hear a girl's voice beside him:

"Oh, what a darling little cat! What's its name?"

"Smokeball," he said, without thinking. "She's about the color of a shrapnel-burst. . . ." Then he stopped short, looking about. There was nobody in sight, and he realized that the voice had been inside his head rather than in his ear.

"What the devil?" he asked himself. "Am I going nuts?"

There was a happy little laugh inside of him, like bubbles rising in a glass of champagne.

"Oh, no; I'm really here," the voice, inaudible but mentally present, assured him. "You can't see me, or touch me, or even really hear me, but I'm not something you just imagined. I'm just as real as . . . as Smokeball, there. Only I'm a different kind of reality. Watch."

The voice stopped, and something that had seemed to be close to him left him. Immediately, the kitten stopped playing with the crumpled paper and cocked her head to one side, staring fixedly as at something above her. He'd seen cats do that before – stare wide-eyed and entranced, as though at something wonderful which was hidden from human eyes. Then, still looking up and to the side, Smokeball trotted over and jumped onto his lap, but even as he stroked her, she was looking at an invisible something beside him. At the same time, he had a warm and pleasant feeling, as of a happy and affectionate presence near him.

"No," he said, slowly and judicially. "That's not just my imagination. But who – or what – are you?"

"I'm. . . . Oh, I don't know how to think it so that you'll understand." The voice inside his head seemed baffled, like a physicist trying to explain atomic energy to a Hottentot. "I'm not material. If you can imagine a mind that doesn't need a brain to think with. . . . Oh, I can't explain it now! But when I'm talking to you, like this, I'm really thinking inside your brain, along with your own mind, and you hear the words without there being any sound. And you just don't know any words that would express it."

He had never thought much, one way or another, about spiritualism. There had been old people, when he had been a boy, who had told stories of ghosts and apparitions, with the firmest conviction that they were true. And there had been an Irishman, in his old company in the Philippines, who swore that the ghost of a dead comrade walked post with him when he was on guard.

"Are you a spirit?" he asked. "I mean, somebody who once lived in a body, like me?"

"N-no." The voice inside him seemed doubtful. "That is, I don't think so. I know about spirits; they're all around, everywhere. But I don't think I'm one. At least, I've always been like I am now, as long as I can remember. Most spirits don't seem to sense me. I can't reach most living people, either; their minds are closed to me, or they have such disgusting minds I can't bear to touch them. Children are open to me, but when they tell their parents about me, they are laughed at, or punished for lying, and then they close up against me. You're the first grown-up person I've been able to reach for a long time."

"Probably getting into my second childhood," Colonel Hampton grunted.

"Oh, but you mustn't be ashamed of that!" the invisible entity told him. "That's the beginning of real wisdom – becoming childlike again. One of your religious teachers said something like that, long ago, and a long time before that, there was a Chinaman whom people called Venerable Child, because his wisdom had turned back again to a child's simplicity."

"That was Lao Tze," Colonel Hampton said, a little surprised. "Don't tell me you've been around that long."

"Oh, but I have! Longer than that; oh, for very long." And yet the voice he seemed to be hearing was the voice of a young girl. "You don't mind my coming to talk to you?" it continued. "I get so lonely, so dreadfully lonely, you see."

"Urmh! So do I," Colonel Hampton admitted. "I'm probably going bats, but what the hell? It's a nice way to go bats, I'll say that. . . . Stick around; whoever you are, and let's get acquainted. I sort of like you."

A feeling of warmth suffused him, as though he had been hugged by someone young and happy and loving.

"Oh, I'm glad. I like you, too; you're nice!"

"Yes, of course." Doctor Vehrner nodded sagely. "That is a schizoid tendency; the flight from reality into a dream-world peopled by creatures of the imagination. You understand, there is usually a mixture of psychotic conditions, in cases like this. We will say that this case begins with simple senile dementia – physical brain degeneration, a result of advanced age. Then the paranoid symptoms appear; he imagines himself surrounded by envious enemies, who are conspiring against him. The patient then withdraws into himself, and in his self-imposed isolation, he conjures up imaginary companionship. I have no doubt. . . ."

In the beginning, he had suspected that this unseen visitor was no more than a figment of his own lonely imagination, but as the days passed, this suspicion vanished. Whatever this entity might be, an entity it was, entirely distinct from his own conscious or subconscious mind.

At first she – he had early come to think of the being as feminine – had seemed timid, fearful lest her intrusions into his mind prove a nuisance. It took some time for him to assure her that she was always welcome. With time, too, his impression of her grew stronger and more concrete. He found that he was able to visualize her, as he might visualize something remembered, or conceived of in imagination – a lovely young girl, slender and clothed in something loose and filmy, with flowers in her honey-colored hair, and clear blue eyes, a pert, cheerful face, a wide, smiling mouth and an impudently up-tilted nose. He realized that this image was merely a sort of allegorical representation, his own private object-abstraction from a reality which his senses could never picture as it existed.

It was about this time that he had begun to call her Dearest. She had given him no name, and seemed quite satisfied with that one.

"I've been thinking," she said, "I ought to have a name for you, too. Do you mind if I call you Popsy?"

"Huh?" He had been really startled at that. If he needed any further proof of Dearest's independent existence, that was it. Never, in the uttermost depths of his subconscious, would he have been likely to label himself Popsy. "Know what they used to call me in the Army?" he asked. "Slaughterhouse Hampton. They claimed I needed a truckload of sawdust to follow me around and cover up the blood." He chuckled. "Nobody but you would think of calling me Popsy."

There was a price, he found, that he must pay for Dearest's companionship – the price of eternal vigilance. He found that he was acquiring the habit of opening doors and then needlessly standing aside to allow her to precede him. And, although she insisted that he need not speak aloud to her, that she could understand any thought which he directed to her, he could not help actually pronouncing the words, if only in a faint whisper. He was glad that he had learned, before the end of his plebe year at West Point, to speak without moving his lips.

Besides himself and the kitten, Smokeball, there was one other at "Greyrock" who was aware, if only faintly, of Dearest's presence. That was old Sergeant Williamson, the Colonel's Negro servant, a retired first sergeant from the regiment he had last commanded. With increasing frequency, he would notice the old Negro pause in his work, as though trying to identify something too subtle for his senses, and then shake his head in bewilderment.

One afternoon in early October – just about a year ago – he had been reclining in a chair on the west veranda, smoking a cigar and trying to re-create, for his companion, a mental picture of an Indian camp as he had seen it in Wyoming in the middle '90's, when Sergeant Williamson came out from the house, carrying a pair of the Colonel's field-boots and a polishing-kit. Unaware of the Colonel's presence, he set down his burden, squatted on the floor and began polishing the boots, humming softly to himself. Then he must have caught a whiff of the Colonel's cigar. Raising his head, he saw the Colonel, and made as though to pick up the boots and polishing equipment.

"Oh, that's all right, Sergeant," the Colonel told him. "Carry on with what you're doing. There's room enough for both of us here."

"Yessuh; thank yo', suh." The old ex-sergeant resumed his soft humming, keeping time with the brush in his hand.

"You know, Popsy, I think he knows I'm here," Dearest said. "Nothing definite, of course; he just feels there's something here that he can't see."

"I wonder. I've noticed something like that. Funny, he doesn't seem to mind, either. Colored people are usually scary about ghosts and spirits and the like. . . . I'm going to ask him." He raised his voice. "Sergeant, do you seem to notice anything peculiar around here, lately?"

The repetitious little two-tone melody broke off short. The soldier-servant lifted his face and looked into the Colonel's. His brow wrinkled, as though he were trying to express a thought for which he had no words.

"Yo' notice dat, too, suh?" he asked. "Why, yessuh, Cunnel; Ah don' know 'zackly how t' say hit, but dey is som'n, at dat. Hit seems like . . . like a kinda . . . a kinda *blessedness.*" He chuckled. "Dat's hit, Cunnel; dey's a blessedness. Wondeh iffen Ah's gittin' r'ligion, now?"

"Well, all this is very interesting, I'm sure, Doctor," T. Barnwell Powell was saying, polishing his glasses on a piece of tissue and keeping one elbow on his briefcase at the same time. "But really, it's not getting us anywhere, so to say. You know, we must have that commitment signed by you. Now, is it or is it not your opinion that this man is of unsound mind?"

"Now, have patience, Mr. Powell," the psychiatrist soothed him. "You must admit that as long as this gentleman refuses to talk, I cannot be said to have interviewed him."

"What if he won't talk?" Stephen Hampton burst out. "We've told you about his behavior; how he sits for hours mumbling to this imaginary person he thinks is with him, and how he always steps aside when he opens a door, to let somebody who isn't there go through ahead of him, and how. . . . Oh, hell, what's the use? If he were in his right mind, he'd speak up and try to prove it, wouldn't he? What do you say, Myra?"

Myra was silent, and Colonel Hampton found himself watching her with interest. Her mouth had twisted into a wry grimace, and she was clutching the arms of her chair until her knuckles whitened. She seemed to be in some intense pain. Colonel Hampton hoped she were; preferably with something slightly fatal.

Sergeant Williamson's suspicion that he might be getting religion became a reality, for a time, that winter, after The Miracle.

It had been a blustery day in mid-January, with a high wind driving swirls of snow across the fields, and Colonel Hampton, fretting indoors for several days, decided to go out and fill his lungs with fresh air. Bundled warmly, swinging his blackthorn cane, he had set out, accompanied by Dearest, to tramp cross-country to the village, three miles from "Greyrock." They had enjoyed the walk through the white windswept desolation, the old man and his invisible companion, until the accident had happened.

A sheet of glassy ice had lain treacherously hidden under a skift of snow; when he stepped upon it, his feet shot from under him, the stick flew from his hand, and he went down. When he tried to rise, he found that he could not. Dearest had been almost frantic.

"Oh, Popsy, you must get up!" she cried. "You'll freeze if you don't. Come on, Popsy; try again!"

He tried, in vain. His old body would not obey his will.

"It's no use, Dearest; I can't. Maybe it's just as well," he said. "Freezing's an easy death, and you say people live on as spirits, after they die. Maybe we can always be together, now."

"I don't know. I don't want you to die yet, Popsy. I never was able to get through to a spirit, and I'm afraid. . . . Wait! Can you crawl a little? Enough to get over under those young pines?"

"I think so." His left leg was numb, and he believed that it was broken. "I can try."

He managed to roll onto his back, with his head toward the clump of pine seedlings. Using both hands and his right heel, he was able to propel himself slowly through the snow until he was out of the worst of the wind.

"That's good; now try to cover yourself," Dearest advised. "Put your hands in your coat pockets. And wait here; I'll try to get help."

Then she left him. For what seemed a long time, he lay motionless in the scant protection of the young pines, suffering miserably. He began to grow drowsy. As soon as he realized what was happening, he was frightened, and the fright pulled him awake again. Soon he felt himself drowsing again. By shifting his position, he caused a jab of pain from his broken leg, which brought him back to wakefulness. Then the deadly drowsiness returned.

This time, he was wakened by a sharp voice, mingled with a throbbing sound that seemed part of a dream of the cannonading in the Argonne.

"Dah! Look-a dah!" It was, he realized, Sergeant Williamson's voice. "Gittin' soft in de haid, is Ah, yo' ol' wuthless no-'count?"

He turned his face, to see the battered jeep from "Greyrock," driven by Arthur, the stableman and gardener, with Sergeant Williamson beside him. The older Negro jumped to the ground and ran toward him. At the same time, he felt Dearest with him again.

"We made it, Popsy! We made it!" she was exulting. "I was afraid I'd never make him understand, but I did. And you should have seen him bully that other man into driving the jeep. Are you all right, Popsy?"

"Is yo' all right, Cunnel?" Sergeant Williamson was asking.

"My leg's broken, I think, but outside of that I'm all right," he answered both of them. "How did you happen to find me, Sergeant?"

The old Negro soldier rolled his eyes upward. "Cunnel, hit war a mi'acle of de blessed Lawd!" he replied, solemnly. "An angel of de Lawd done appeahed unto me." He shook his head slowly. "Ah's a sinful man,

Cunnel; Ah couldn't see de angel face to face, but de glory of de angel was befoh me, an' guided me."

They used his cane and a broken-off bough to splint the leg; they wrapped him in a horse-blanket and hauled him back to "Greyrock" and put him to bed, with Dearest clinging solicitously to him. The fractured leg knit slowly, though the physician was amazed at the speed with which, considering his age, he made recovery, and with his unfailing cheerfulness. He did not know, of course, that he was being assisted by an invisible nurse. For all that, however, the leaves on the oaks around "Greyrock" were green again before Colonel Hampton could leave his bed and hobble about the house on a cane.

Arthur, the young Negro who had driven the jeep, had become one of the most solid pillars of the little A.M.E. church beyond the village, as a result. Sergeant Williamson had also become an attendant at church for a while, and then stopped. Without being able to define, or spell, or even pronounce the term, Sergeant Williamson was a strict pragmatist. Most Africans are, even five generations removed from the slave-ship that brought their forefathers from the Dark Continent. And Sergeant Williamson could not find the blessedness at the church. Instead, it seemed to center about the room where his employer and former regiment commander lay. That, to his mind, was quite reasonable. If an Angel of the Lord was going to tarry upon earth, the celestial being would naturally prefer the society of a retired U.S.A. colonel to that of a passel of triflin', no-'counts at an ol' clapboard church house. Be that as it may, he could always find the blessedness in Colonel Hampton's room, and sometimes, when the Colonel would be asleep, the blessedness would follow him out and linger with him for a while.

Colonel Hampton wondered, anxiously, where Dearest was, now. He had not felt her presence since his nephew had brought his lawyer and the psychiatrist into the house. He wondered if she had voluntarily separated herself from him for fear he might give her some sign of recognition that these harpies would fasten upon as an evidence of unsound mind. He could not believe that she had deserted him entirely, now when he needed her most. . . .

"Well, what can I do?" Doctor Vehrner was complaining. "You bring me here to interview him, and he just sits there and does nothing. . . . Will you consent to my giving him an injection of sodium pentathol?"

"Well, I don't know, now," T. Barnwell Powell objected. "I've heard of that drug – one of the so-called 'truth-serum' drugs. I doubt if testimony taken under its influence would be admissible in a court. . . ."

"This is not a court, Mr. Powell," the doctor explained patiently. "And I am not taking testimony; I am making a diagnosis. Pentathol is a recognized diagnostic agent."

"Go ahead," Stephen Hampton said. "Anything to get this over with. . . . You agree, Myra?"

Myra said nothing. She simply sat, with staring eyes, and clutched the arms of her chair as though to keep from slipping into some dreadful abyss. Once a low moan escaped from her lips.

"My wife is naturally overwrought by this painful business," Stephen said. "I trust that you gentlemen will excuse her. . . . Hadn't you better go and lie down somewhere, Myra?"

She shook her head violently, moaning again. Both the doctor and the attorney were looking at her curiously.

"Well, I object to being drugged," Colonel Hampton said, rising. "And what's more, I won't submit to it."

"Albert!" Doctor Vehrner said sharply, nodding toward the Colonel. The pithecanthropoid attendant in the white jacket hastened forward, pinned his arms behind him and dragged him down into the chair. For an instant, the old man tried to resist, then, realizing the futility and undignity of struggling, subsided. The psychiatrist had taken a leather case from his pocket and was selecting a hypodermic needle.

Then Myra Hampton leaped to her feet, her face working hideously. "No! Stop! Stop!" she cried.

Everybody looked at her in surprise, Colonel Hampton no less than the others. Stephen Hampton called out her name sharply.

"No! You shan't do this to me! You shan't! You're torturing me! you are all devils!" she screamed. "Devils! *Devils!*"

"Myra!" her husband barked, stepping forward.

With a twist, she eluded him, dashing around the desk and pulling open a drawer.

For an instant, she fumbled inside it, and when she brought her hand up, she had Colonel Hampton's .45 automatic in it. She drew back the slide and released it, loading the chamber.

Doctor Vehrner, the hypodermic in his hand, turned. Stephen Hampton sprang at her, dropping his drink. And Albert, the prognathous attendant, released Colonel Hampton and leaped at the woman with the pistol, with the unthinking promptness of a dog whose master is in danger.

Stephen Hampton was the closest to her; she shot him first, point-blank in the chest. The heavy bullet knocked him backward against a small table; he and it fell over together. While he was falling, the woman turned, dipped the muzzle of her pistol slightly and fired again; Doctor Vehrner's leg gave way under him and he went down, the hypodermic flying from his hand and landing at Colonel Hampton's feet. At the same time, the attendant, Albert, was almost upon her. Quickly, she reversed the heavy Colt, pressed the muzzle against her heart, and fired a third shot.

T. Barnwell Powell had let the briefcase slip to the floor; he was staring, slack-jawed, at the tableau of violence which had been enacted before him. The attendant, having reached Myra, was looking down at her stupidly. Then he stooped, and straightened.

"She's dead!" he said, unbelievingly.

Colonel Hampton rose, putting his heel on the hypodermic and crushing it.

"Of course she's dead!" he barked. "You have any first-aid training? Then look after these other people. Doctor Vehrner first; the other man's unconscious; he'll wait."

"No; look after the other man first," Doctor Vehrner said.

Albert gaped back and forth between them.

"Goddamnit, you heard me!" Colonel Hampton roared. It was Slaughterhouse Hampton, whose service-ribbons started with the Indian campaigns, speaking; an officer who never for an instant imagined that his orders would not be obeyed. "Get a tourniquet on that man's leg, you!" He moderated his voice and manner about half a degree and spoke to Vehrner. "You are not the doctor, you're the patient, now. You'll do as you're told. Don't you know that a man shot in the leg with a .45 can bleed to death without half trying?"

"Yo'-all do like de Cunnel says, 'r foh Gawd, yo'-all gwine wish yo' had," Sergeant Williamson said, entering the room. "Git a move on."

He stood just inside the doorway, holding a silver-banded Malacca walking-stick that he had taken from the hall-stand. He was grasping it in his left hand, below the band, with the crook out, holding it at his side as though it were a sword in a scabbard, which was exactly what that walking-stick was. Albert looked at him, and then back at Colonel Hampton. Then, whipping off his necktie, he went down on his knees beside Doctor Vehrner, skillfully applying the improvised tourniquet, twisting it tight with an eighteen-inch ruler the Colonel took from the desk and handed to him.

"Go get the first-aid kit, Sergeant," the Colonel said. "And hurry. Mr. Stephen's been shot, too."

"Yessuh!" Sergeant Williamson executed an automatic salute and about-face and raced from the room. The Colonel picked up the telephone on the desk.

The County Hospital was three miles from "Greyrock"; the State Police substation a good five. He dialed the State Police number first.

"Sergeant Mallard? Colonel Hampton, at 'Greyrock.' We've had a little trouble here. My nephew's wife just went *juramentado* with one of my pistols, shot and wounded her husband and another man, and then shot and killed herself. . . . Yes, indeed it is, Sergeant. I wish you'd send somebody over here, as soon as possible, to take charge. . . . Oh, you will? That's good. . . . No, it's all over, and nobody to arrest; just the formalities. . . . Well, thank you, Sergeant."

The old Negro cavalryman reentered the room, without the sword-cane and carrying a heavy leather box on a strap over his shoulder. He set this on the floor and opened it, then knelt beside Stephen Hampton. The Colonel was calling the hospital.

". . . gunshot wounds," he was saying. "One man in the chest and the other in the leg, both with a .45 pistol. And you'd better send a doctor who's qualified to write a death certificate; there was a woman killed, too. . . . Yes, certainly; the State Police have been notified."

"Dis ain' so bad, Cunnel," Sergeant Williamson raised his head to say. "Ah's seen men shot wuss'n dis dat was ma'ked 'Duty' inside a month, suh."

Colonel Hampton nodded. "Well, get him fixed up as best you can, till the ambulance gets here. And there's whiskey and glasses on that table, over there. Better give Doctor Vehrner a drink." He looked at T. Barnwell Powell, still frozen to his chair, aghast at the carnage around him. "And give Mr. Powell a drink, too. He needs one."

He did, indeed. Colonel Hampton could have used a drink, too; the library looked like beef-day at an Indian agency. But he was still Slaughterhouse Hampton, and consequently could not afford to exhibit queasiness.

It was then, for the first time since the business had started that he felt the presence of Dearest.

"Oh, Popsy, are you all right?" the voice inside his head was asking. "It's all over, now; you won't have anything to worry about, anymore. But, oh, I was afraid I wouldn't be able to do it!"

"My God, Dearest!" He almost spoke aloud. "Did you make her do that?"

"Popsy!" The voice in his mind was grief-stricken. "You. . . . You're afraid of me! Never be afraid of Dearest, Popsy! And don't hate me for this. It was the only thing I could do. If he'd given you that injection, he could have made you tell him all about us, and then he'd have been sure you were crazy, and they'd have taken you away. And they treat people dreadfully at that place of his. You'd have been driven really crazy before long, and then your mind would have been closed to me, so that I wouldn't have been able to get through to you, anymore. What I did was the only thing I could do."

"I don't hate you, Dearest," he replied, mentally. "And I don't blame you. It was a little disconcerting, though, to discover the extent of your capabilities. . . . How did you manage it?"

"You remember how I made the Sergeant see an angel, the time you were down in the snow?" Colonel Hampton nodded. "Well, I made her see . . . things that weren't angels," Dearest continued. "After I'd driven her almost to distraction, I was able to get into her mind and take control of her." Colonel Hampton felt a shudder inside of him. "That was horrible; that woman had a mind like a sewer; I still feel dirty from it! But I made her get the pistol – I knew where you kept it – and I knew how to use it, even if she didn't. Remember when we were shooting muskrats, that time, along the river?"

"Uhuh. I wondered how she knew enough to unlock the action and load the chamber." He turned and faced the others.

Doctor Vehrner was sitting on the floor, with his back to the chair Colonel Hampton had occupied, his injured leg stretched out in front of him. Albert was hovering over him with mother-hen solicitude. T. Barnwell Powell was finishing his whiskey and recovering a fraction of his normal poise.

"Well, I suppose you gentlemen see, now, who was really crazy around here?" Colonel Hampton addressed them bitingly. "That woman has been dangerously close to the borderline of sanity for as long as she's been here. I think my precious nephew trumped up this ridiculous insanity complaint against me as much to discredit any testimony I might ever give about his wife's mental condition as because he wanted to get control of my estate. I also suppose that the tension she was under here, this afternoon, was too much for her, and the scheme boomeranged on its originators. Curious case of poetic justice, but I'm sorry you had to be included in it, Doctor."

"Attaboy, Popsy!" Dearest enthused. "Now you have them on the run; don't give them a chance to re-form. You know what Patton always said – Grab 'em by the nose and kick 'em in the pants."

Colonel Hampton re-lighted his cigar. "Patton only said 'pants' when he was talking for publication," he told her, *sotto voce.* Then he noticed the unsigned commitment paper lying on the desk. He picked it up, crumpled it, and threw it into the fire.

"I don't think you'll be needing that," he said. "You know, this isn't the first time my loving nephew has expressed doubts as to my sanity." He sat down in the chair at the desk, motioning to his servant to bring him a drink. "And see to the other gentlemen's glasses, Sergeant," he directed. "Back in 1929, Stephen thought I was crazy as a bedbug to sell all my securities and take a paper loss, around the first of September. After October 24th, I bought them back at about twenty percent of what I'd sold them for, after he'd lost his shirt." That, he knew, would have an effect on T. Barnwell Powell. "And in December, 1944, I was just plain nuts, selling all my munition shares and investing in a company that manufactured baby-food. Stephen thought that Rundstedt's Ardennes counter-offensive would put off the end of the war for another year and a half!"

"Baby-food, eh?" Doctor Vehrner chuckled.

Colonel Hampton sipped his whiskey slowly, then puffed on his cigar. "No, this pair were competent liars," he replied. "A good workmanlike liar never makes up a story out of the whole cloth; he always takes a fabric of truth and embroiders it to suit the situation." He smiled grimly; that was an accurate description of his own tactical procedure at the moment. "I hadn't intended this to come out, Doctor, but it happens that I am a convinced believer in spiritualism. I suppose you'll think that's a delusional belief, too?"

"Well. . . ." Doctor Vehrner pursed his lips. "I reject the idea of survival after death, myself, but I think that people who believe in such a theory are merely misevaluating evidence. It is definitely not, in itself, a symptom of a psychotic condition."

"Thank you, Doctor." The Colonel gestured with his cigar. "Now, I'll admit their statements about my appearing to be in conversation with some invisible or imaginary being. That's all quite true. I'm convinced that I'm in direct-voice communication with the spirit of a young girl who was killed by Indians in this section about a hundred and seventy-five years ago. At first, she communicated by automatic writing; later we established direct-voice communication. Well, naturally, a man in my position would dislike the label of spirit-medium; there are too many invidious associations connected with the term. But there it is. I trust both of you gentlemen will remember the ethics of your respective professions and keep this confidential."

"Oh, brother!" Dearest was fairly hugging him with delight. "When bigger and better lies are told, we tell them, don't we, Popsy?"

"Yes, and try and prove otherwise," Colonel Hampton replied, around his cigar. Then he blew a jet of smoke and spoke to the men in front of him.

"I intend paying for my nephew's hospitalization, and for his wife's funeral," he said. "And then, I'm going to pack up all his personal belongings, and all of hers; when he's discharged from the hospital, I'll ship them wherever he wants them. But he won't be allowed to come back here. After this business, I'm through with him."

T. Barnwell Powell nodded primly. "I don't blame you, in the least, Colonel," he said. "I think you have been abominably treated, and your attitude is most generous." He was about to say something else, when the doorbell tinkled and Sergeant Williamson went out into the hall. "Oh, dear; I suppose that's the police, now," the lawyer said. He grimaced like a small boy in a dentist's chair.

Colonel Hampton felt Dearest leave him for a moment. Then she was back.

"The ambulance." Then he caught a sparkle of mischief in her mood. "Let's have some fun, Popsy! The doctor is a young man, with brown hair and a mustache, horn-rimmed glasses, a blue tie and a tan-leather bag. One of the ambulance men has red hair, and the other has a mercurochrome-stain on his left sleeve. Tell them your spirit-guide told you."

The old soldier's tobacco-yellowed mustache twitched with amusement.

"No, gentlemen, it is the ambulance," he corrected. "My spirit-control says. . . ." He relayed Dearest's descriptions to them.

T. Barnwell Powell blinked. A speculative look came into the psychiatrist's eyes; he was probably wishing the commitment paper hadn't been destroyed.

Then the doctor came bustling in, brown-mustached, blue-tied, spectacled, carrying a tan bag, and behind him followed the two ambulance men, one with a thatch of flaming red hair and the other with a stain of mercurochrome on his jacket-sleeve.

For an instant, the lawyer and the psychiatrist gaped at them. Then T. Barnwell Powell put one hand to his mouth and made a small gibbering sound, and Doctor Vehrner gave a faint squawk, and then both men grabbed, simultaneously, for the whiskey bottle.

The laughter of Dearest tinkled inaudibly through the rumbling mirth of Colonel Hampton.

THE END

The Return

By H. BEAM PIPER *and* JOHN J. McGUIRE

I

Altamont cast a quick, routine glance at the instrument panels and then looked down through the transparent nose of the helicopter at the yellow-brown river five hundred feet below. Next he scraped the last morsel from his plate and ate it.

"What did you make this out of, Jim?" he asked. "I hope you kept notes while you were concocting it. It's good."

"The two smoked pork chops left over from yesterday evening," Loudons said, "and that bowl of rice that's been taking up space in the refrigerator the last couple of days, together with a little egg powder and some milk. I ground the chops up and mixed them with the rice and other stuff. Then added some bacon, to make grease to fry it in."

Altamont chuckled. That was Loudons, all right: he could take a few leftovers, mess them together, pop them in the skillet, and have a meal that would turn the chef back at the Fort green with envy. He filled his cup and offered the pot.

"Caffchoc?" he asked.

Loudons held his cup out to be filled, blew on it, sipped, and then hunted on the ledge under the desk for the butt of the cigar he had half-smoked the evening before.

"Did you ever drink coffee, Monty?" the socio-psychologist asked, getting the cigar drawing to his taste.

"Coffee? No. I've read about it, of course. We'll have to organize an expedition to Brazil, sometime, to get seeds and try raising some."

Loudons blew a smoke ring toward the rear of the cabin.

"A much overrated beverage," he replied. "We found some, once, when I was on that expedition into Idaho, in what must have been the stockroom of a hotel. Vacuum-packed in moisture-proof containers, and free from radioactivity. It wasn't nearly as good as caffchoc.

"But then, I suppose, a pre-bustup coffee drinker couldn't stomach this stuff we're drinking."

Loudons looked forward, up the river they were following. "Get anything on the radio?" he asked. "I noticed you took us up to about ten thousand, while I was shaving."

Altamont got out his pipe and tobacco pouch, filling the former slowly and carefully.

"Not a whisper. I tried Colony Three, in the Ozarks, and I tried to call in that tribe of workers in Louisiana. I couldn't get either."

"Maybe if we tried to get a little more power on the set. . . ."

That was Loudons, too, Altamont thought. There wasn't a better man at the Fort, when it came to dealing with people. But confront him with a problem about things and he was lost.

That was one of the reasons why he and the stocky, phlegmatic social scientist made such a good team, he thought. As far as he, himself, was concerned, people were just a mysterious, exasperatingly unpredictable order of things which were subject to no known natural laws.

And Loudons thought the same thing about machines: he couldn't psychoanalyze them.

Altamont gestured with his pipe toward the nuclear-electric conversion unit, between the control-cabin and the living quarters in the rear of the boxcar-sized helicopter.

"We have enough power back there to keep this windmill in the air twenty-four hours a day, three hundred and sixty-five days a year, for the next fifteen years," he said. "We just don't have enough radio. If I'd step up the power on this set anymore, it'd burn out before I could say, 'Altamont calling Fort Ridgeway.'"

"How far are we from Pittsburgh now?" Loudons wanted to know.

Altamont looked across the cabin at the big map of the United States as they had been, the red and green and blue and yellow patchwork of vanished political divisions. The colors gleamed through the transparent overlay on which this voyage of re-discovery was plotted.

The red line of their journey started at Fort Ridgeway, in what had been Arizona. It angled east by a little north, to Colony Three, in northern Arkansas . . . sharply northeast to St. Louis and its lifeless ruins . . . then to Chicago and Gary, where little bands of Stone Age reversions stalked and fought and ate each other . . . Detroit, where things that had completely forgotten they were human emerged from their burrows only at night . . . Cleveland, where a couple of cobalt bombs must have landed in the lake and drenched everything with radioactivity that still lingered after two centuries . . . Akron, where vegetation was only beginning to break through the glassy slag . . . Cincinnati, where they had last stopped. . . .

"How's the leg this morning, Jim?" he asked.

"Little stiff. Doesn't hurt much, though."

"Why, we're about fifty miles, as we follow that river, and that's relatively straight." He looked down through the transparent nose of the copter at a town, now choked with trees that grew among the tumbled walls. "I think that's Aliquippa."

Loudons looked and shrugged, then looked again and pointed.

"There's a bear. Just ducked into that church or movie theater or whatever. I wonder what he thinks we are."

Altamont puffed slowly at his pipe. "I wonder if we're going to find anything at all in Pittsburgh."

"You mean people, as distinct from those biped beasts we've found so far? I doubt it," Loudons replied, finishing his caffchoc and wiping his mustache with the back of his hand. "I think the whole eastern half of the country is nothing but forest like this, and the highest type of life is just about three cuts below Homo Neanderthalensis, almost impossible to contact, and even more impossible to educate."

"I wasn't thinking about that. I've just about given up hope of finding anybody or even a reasonably high level of barbarism," Altamont said. "I was thinking about that cache of microfilmed books that was buried at the Carnegie Library."

"*If* it was buried," Loudons qualified. "All we have is that article in that two-century-old copy of *Time* about how the people at the library had constructed the crypt and were beginning the microfilming. We don't know if they ever had a chance to get it finished, before the rockets started landing."

They passed over a dam of flotsam that had banked up at a wrecked bridge and accumulated enough mass to resist the periodic floods that had kept the river usually clear. Three human figures fled across a sand-flat at one end of it and disappeared into the woods. Two of them carried spears tipped with something that sparkled in the sunlight, probably shards of glass.

"You know, Monty, I get nightmares, sometimes, thinking about what things must be like in Europe," Loudons said.

Five or six wild cows went crashing through the brush below. Altamont nodded when he saw them.

"Maybe tomorrow, we'll let down and shoot a cow," he said. "I was looking in the freeze-locker and the fresh meat's getting a little low. Or a wild pig, if we find a good stand of oak trees. I could enjoy what you'd do with some acorn-fed pork."

He looked across the table. "Finished?" he asked Loudons. "Take over, then. I'll go back and wash the dishes."

They rose, and Loudons, favoring his left leg, moved over to the seat at the controls.

Altamont gathered up the two cups, the stainless-steel dishes, and the knives and the forks and spoons, going up the steps over the shielded converter and ducking his head to avoid the seat in the forward top machine-gun turret. He washed and dried the dishes, noting with satisfaction that the gauge of the water tank was still reasonably high, and glanced out one of the windows. Loudons was taking the big helicopter upstairs, for a better view.

Now and then, among the trees, there would be a glint of glassy slag, usually in a fairly small circle. That was to be expected: beside the three or four H-bombs that had fallen on the Pittsburgh area, mentioned in the transcripts of the last news to reach the Fort from the outside, the whole district had been pelted, more or less at random, with fission bombs.

West of the confluence of the Allegheny and the Monongahela, it would probably be worse than this.

"Can you see Pittsburgh yet, Jim?" he called out.

"Yes, it's a mess! Worse than Gary, worse than Akron even."

"Monty! Come here! I think I have something!"

Picking up the pipe he had laid down, Altamont hurried forward, dodging his six-foot length under the gun turret and swinging down from the walkway over the converter.

"What is it?" he asked.

"Smoke. A lot of smoke, twenty or thirty fires at the very least."

Loudons had shifted from Forward to Hover and was peering through a pair of binoculars. "See that island, the long one? Across the river from it, on the north side, toward this end. Yes, by Einstein! And I can see cleared ground, and what I think are houses, inside a stockade. . . ."

II

Murray Hughes walked around the corner of the cabin into the morning sunlight, lacing his trousers, with his hunting shirt thrown over his bare shoulders. He found, without much surprise, that his father had also slept late. Verner Hughes was just beginning to shave.

Inside the kitchen, his mother and the girls were clattering pots and skillets.

Outside the kitchen door, his younger brother, Hector, was noisily chopping wood.

Going through the door, he filled another of the light-metal basins with hot water, found his razor, and went outside again, setting the basin on the bench.

Most of the ware in the Hughes cabin was of light-metal. Murray and his father had mined it in the dead city up the river, from a place where it had floated to the top of a puddle of slag, back when the city had been blasted, at the end of the hard times.

It had been hard work, but the stuff had been easy to carry down to where they had hidden their boat. And, for once, they'd had no trouble with the Scowrers.

Too bad they couldn't say as much for yesterday's hunting trip!

As he rubbed lather into the stubble on his face, he cursed with irritation. That had been a bad-luck hunt, all around.

They had gone out before dawn, hunting into the hills to the north. They'd spent the day at it, and shot one small wild pig. Lucky it was small, at that. They'd have had to abandon a full-grown one, after the Scowrers had began hunting them. Six of them, as big a band as he'd ever seen together at one time, had managed to cut them off from the stockade. He and his father had been forced to circle miles out of their way.

His father had shot one, and he'd had to leave his hatchet sticking in the skull of another, when his rifle had misfired.

That meant a trip to the gunsmith's, for a new hatchet and to have the mainspring of the rifle replaced. Nobody could afford to have a rifle that couldn't be trusted, least of all a hunter and prospector.

On top of everything else, he had had a few words with Alex Barrett, the gunsmith, the other day.

Well, at least that could be smoothed over. Barrett would be glad to do business with him, once the gunsmith saw that hard tool-steel he had dug out of that place down the river. Hardest steel either he or his father had ever found, and it hadn't been atom-spoiled, either.

He cleaned, wiped and stropped his razor and put it back in the case. He threw out the wash-water on the compost pile and went into the cabin, putting on his shirt and his belt. Then he passed through to the front porch, where his father was already eating at the table.

The people of the Toon like to eat in the open. It was something they'd always done, just as they'd always like to eat together in the evenings.

He sweetened his cup of chicory with a lump of maple sugar and began to sip it before he sat down, standing with one foot on the bench and looking down across the parade ground, past the Aitch-Cue House, toward the river and the wall.

"If you're coming around to Alex's way of thinking – and mine – it won't hurt you to admit it, son," his father said.

Murray turned, looking at his father with the beginning of anger, and then he grinned. The elders were constantly keeping the young men alert with these tests. He checked back over his actions since he had come out onto the porch.

. . . to the table, sugar in his chicory, one foot on the bench . . . which had reminded him again of the absence of the hatchet from his belt and brought an automatic frown . . . then the glance toward the gunsmith's shop, and across the parade ground . . . the glance including the houses into which so much labor had gone, the wall that had been built from rubble and topped with pointed stakes, the white slabs of marble that marked the graves of the First Tenant and the men of the Old Toon. . . .

He had thought, at that moment, that maybe his father and Alex Barrett and Reader Rawson and Tenant Mycroft Jones and the others were right: there were too many things here that could not be moved along with them, if they decided to move.

It would be false modesty, refusal to see things as they were, not to admit that he was the leader of the younger men, and the boys of the Irregulars. He had been forced to face the responsibilities of that fact since last winter.

Then, the usual theological arguments about the proper order of the Sacred Books and the true nature of the Risen One had been replaced by a violent controversy when Sholto Jiminez and Birdy Edwards had reopened the old question of the advisability of moving the Toon and settling elsewhere.

He had been in favor of the idea himself and found that the other young men had followed his lead. But, for the last month or so, he had begun to doubt the wisdom of it.

It was probably reluctance to admit this to himself that had brought on the strained feelings between himself and his old friend, the gunsmith.

"I'll have to drill the Irregulars, today," he said. "Birdy Edwards has been drilling them while we've been hunting. But I'll go up and see Alex about a new hatchet and fixing my rifle. I'll have a talk with him."

He stepped forward to the edge of the porch, still munching on a honey-dipped piece of cornbread, and glanced up at the sky. That was a queer bird; he had never seen a bird with a wing action like that.

Then he realized that the object was not a bird at all.

His father was staring at it, too.

"Murray! That's . . . that's like the old stories from the time of the wars!"

But Murray was already racing across the parade ground toward the Aitch-Cue House, where the big iron ring hung by its chain from a gallowslike post, with a hammer beside it.

III

The stockaded village became larger, details grew plainer, as the helicopter came slanting down and began spiraling around it.

It was a fairly big place, some forty or fifty acres in a rough parallelogram, surrounded by a wall of varicolored stone and brick and concrete rubble from old ruins, topped with a palisade of pointed poles. There was a small jetty projecting into the river, to which six or eight boats of different sorts were tied; a gate opened onto this from the wall.

Inside the stockade, there were close to a hundred buildings, ranging from small cabins to a structure with a belfry. It seemed to have been a church, partly ruined in the war of two centuries ago and later rebuilt.

A stream came down from the woods, across the cultivated land around the fortified village. There was a rough flume which carried the water from a dam close to the edge of the forest and provided a fall to turn a mill wheel.

"Look, strip farming," Loudons pointed. "See the alternate strips of grass and plowed ground. These people understand soil conservation.

"They have horses, too."

As he spoke, three riders left the village at a gallop. They separated, and the people in the fields, who had all started for the village, turned and began hurrying toward the woods. Two of the riders headed for a pasture in which cattle had been grazing and started herding them also into the woods.

For a while, there was a scurrying of little figures in the village below. Then, not a moving thing was in sight.

"There's good organization," Loudons said. "Everybody seems to know what to do, and how to get it done promptly. And look how neat the whole place is. Policed up. I'll bet anything we'll find that they have a military organization, or a military tradition at least.

"We'll have a lot to find out: you can't understand a people until you understand their background and their social organization."

"Humph. Let me have a look at their artifacts: that will tell what kind of people they are," Altamont said, swinging the glasses back and forth over the enclosure. "Water-power mill, water-power sawmill – building on the left side of the water wheel, see the pile of fresh lumber beside it. Blacksmith shop, and from that chimney, I'd say a small foundry, too.

"Wonder what that little building out on the tip of the island is, it has a water wheel too. Undershot wheel, and it looks like it could be raised or lowered. Now, I wonder. . . ."

"Monty, I think we ought to land right in the middle of the enclosure, on that open plaza thing, in front of the building that looks like a reconditioned church. That's probably the Royal Palace, or the Pentagon, or the Kremlin, or whatever."

Altamont started to object, paused, and then nodded. "I think you're right, Jim. From the way they scattered, and got their livestock into the woods, they probably expect us to bomb them. We have to get inside and that's the quickest way to do it." He thought for a moment. "We'd better be armed, when we go out. Pistols, auto-carbines, and a few of those concussion-grenades in case we have to break up a concerted attack. I'll get them."

The plaza, the houses and the cabins around it, the two-hundred-year-old church, all were silent and apparently lifeless as they set the helicopter down. Once Loudons caught a movement inside the door of a house, and saw a metallic glint.

"There's a gun up there," he said. "Looks like a four-pounder. Brass. I knew that smith-shop was also a foundry. See that little curl of smoke? That's the gunner's slow-match.

"I'd thought maybe that thing on the island was a powder mill. That would be where they'd put it. Probably extract their niter from the dung of their horses and cows. Sulfur probably from coal-mine drainage.

"Jim, this is really something!"

"I hope they don't cut loose with that thing," Loudons said, looking apprehensively at the brass-rimmed black muzzle that was covering them from the belfry. "I wonder if we ought to – Oh-oh, here they come!"

Three or four young men stepped out of the wide door of the old church. They wore fringed buckskin trousers and buckskin shirts and odd caps of deerskin with visors to shade the eyes and similar beaks behind to protect the neck. They had powder horns and bullet pouches slung over their shoulders, and long rifles in their hands. They stepped aside as soon as they were out. Carefully avoiding any gesture of menace, they simply stood, watching the helicopter which had landed in their village.

Three other men followed them out. They, too, wore buckskins and the odd double-visored caps. One had a close-cropped white beard, and on the shoulders of his buckskin shirt, he wore the single silver bars of a first lieutenant of the vanished United States Army. He had a pistol on his belt. The pistol had the saw-handle grip of an automatic, but it was a flintlock, as were the rifles of the young men who stood so watchfully on either side of the door.

Two middle-aged men accompanied the bearded man and the trio advanced toward the helicopter.

"All right, come on, Monty."

Loudons opened the door and let down the steps. Picking up an auto-carbine, he slung it and stepped out of the helicopter, Altamont behind him. They advanced to meet the party from the church, halting when they were about twenty feet apart.

"I must apologize, lieutenant, for dropping in on you so unceremoniously."

Loudons stopped, wondering if the man with the white beard understood a word of what he was saying.

"The natural way to come in, when you travel in the air," the old man replied. "At least, you came in openly. I can promise you a better reception than that you got at the city to the west of us a couple of days ago."

"Now how did you know that we had trouble the day-before-yesterday?" Loudons demanded.

The old man's eyes sparkled with childlike pleasure. "That surprises you, my dear sir? In a moment, I daresay you'll be surprised at the simplicity of it.

"You have a nasty rip in the left leg of your trousers, and the cloth around it is stained with blood. Through the rip, I perceive a bandage. Obviously, you have suffered a recent wound. I further observe that the side of your flying machine bears recent scratches, as though from the spears or throwing hatchets of the Scowrers. Evidently, they attacked you as you were landing. It is fortunate that these cannibal devils are too stupid and too anxious for human flesh to exercise patience."

"Well, that explains how you knew that we'd recently been attacked," Loudons told him. "But how did you guess that it had been to the west of here, in a ruined city?"

"I never guess," the oldster with the silver bar and the keystone-shaped red patch on his left shoulder replied. "It is a shocking habit – destructive to the logical faculties. What seems strange to you is only so because you do not follow my train of thought.

"For example, the wheels and their framework under your flying machine are splashed with mud which seems to be predominantly brick-dust, mixed with plaster. Obviously, you landed recently in a dead city, either during or after a rain. There was a rain here yesterday evening, the wind being from the west. Obviously, you followed behind the rain as it came up the river. And now that I look at your boots, I see traces of the same sort of mud, around the soles and in front of the heels.

"But this is heartless of us, keeping you standing here on a wounded leg, sir. Come in, and let our medic take a look at it."

"Well, thank you, lieutenant," Loudons replied. "But don't bother your medic. I've attended to the wound myself, and it wasn't serious to begin with."

"You are a doctor?" the white-haired man asked.

"Of sorts. A sort of general scientist. My name is Loudons. My friend, Mr. Altamont, here, is a scientist, too."

There was an immediate reaction: all three of the elders of the village, and the young riflemen who had accompanied them, exchanged glances of surprise.

Loudons dropped his hand to the grip of his slung auto-carbine and Altamont sidled away from his partner, his hand moving as if by accident toward the butt of his pistol. The same thought was in both men's minds, that these people might feel, as the heritage of the war of two centuries ago, a hostility to science and scientists.

There was no hostility, however, in their manner as the old man came forward with outstretched hand.

"I am Tenant Mycroft Jones, the Toon Leader here," he said. "This is Stamford Rawson, our Reader, and Verner Hughes, our Toon Sarge. This is his son, Murray Hughes, the Toon Sarge of the Irregulars.

"But come into the Aitch-Cue House, gentlemen. We have much to talk about."

By this time, the villagers had begun to emerge from the log cabins and rubble-walled houses around the plaza and the old church. Some of them, mostly the young men, were carrying rifles, but the majority were unarmed. About half of them were women, in short deerskin skirts or homespun dresses. There were a number of children, the younger ones almost completely naked.

"Sarge," the old man told one of the youths, "post a guard over this flying machine. Don't let anybody meddle with it. And have all the noncoms and techs report here, on the double." He turned and shouted up at the truncated steeple: "Atherton, sound 'All Clear!'"

A horn up in the belfry began blowing, apparently to advise the people who had run from the fields into the forest that there was no danger.

They went through the open doorway of the old stone church and entered the big room inside. The building had evidently once been gutted by fire, two centuries ago, but portions of the wall had been restored. The floor had been replaced by one of rough planks, and there was a plank ceiling at about ten feet.

The room was apparently used as a community center. There were a number of benches and chairs, all very neatly made; and along one wall, out of the way, ten or fifteen long tables had been stacked, the tops in a pile and the trestles on the tops.

The walls were decorated with trophies of weapons – a number of M-12 rifles and M-16 submachine-guns, all in good, clean condition; a light machine rifle; two bazookas. Among them were cruder weapons, stone-and metal-tipped spears and clubs, the work of the wild men of the woods.

A stairway led to the second floor, and it was up this stairway that the man who bore the title of Toon Leader conducted them, to a small room furnished with a long table, a number of chairs, and several big wooden chests bound with iron.

"Sit down, gentlemen," the Toon Leader invited, going to a cupboard and producing a large bottle stoppered with a corncob and a number of small cups.

"It's a little early in the day," he went on, "but this is a very special occasion.

"You smoke a pipe, I take it?" he asked Altamont. "Then try some of this, of our own growth and curing."

He extended a doeskin moccasin, which seemed to be the tobacco container.

Altamont looked at the thing dubiously, then filled his pipe from it.

The oldster drew his pistol, pushed a little wooden plug into the vent, added some tow to the priming, and, aiming at the wall, snapped it. Evidently, at time the formality of plugging the vent had been overlooked: there were a number of holes in the wall there.

This time, however, the pistol didn't go off. The old man shook out the smoldering tow, blew it into flame, and lit a candle from it, offering the light to Altamont.

Loudons got out a cigar and lit it from the candle; the others filled and lighted pipes. The Toon Leader reprimed his pistol, then holstered it, took off his belt and laid it aside, an example the others followed.

They drank ceremoniously, and then seated themselves at the table. As they did, two more men entered the room. They were introduced as Alexander Barrett, the gunsmith and Stanley Markovitch, the distiller.

The Toon Leader began by asking, "You come, then, from the west?"

"Are you from Utah?" the gunsmith interrupted, suspiciously.

"Why, no, we're from Arizona. A place called Fort Ridgeway," Loudons said.

The others nodded, in the manner of people who wish to conceal ignorance. It was obvious that none of them had ever heard of Fort Ridgeway, or Arizona either.

"You say you come from a fort? Then the wars aren't over yet?" Sarge Hughes asked.

"The wars have been over for a long time. You know how terrible they were. You know how few in all the countries were left alive," Loudons said.

"None that we know of, beside ourselves and the Scowrers, until you came," the Toon Leader said.

"We have found only a few small groups, in the whole country, who have managed to save anything of the Old Times. Most of them lived in little villages and cultivated land. A few had horses or cows. None, that we have ever found before, made guns and powder for themselves. But they remembered that they were men, and did not eat one another.

"Whenever we find a group of people like this, we try to persuade them to let us help them."

"Why?" the Toon Leader asked. "Why do you do this for people that you have never met before? What do you want from them – from us – in return for your help?"

He was speaking to Altamont, rather than to Loudons. It seemed obvious that he believed Altamont to be the leader and Loudons the subordinate.

"Because we are trying to bring back the best of the Old Times," Altamont told him. "Look, you have had troubles, here. So have we, many times. Years when the crops didn't . . . didn't. . . ." He looked at Loudons, aware that his partner should be talking now, and also suddenly aware that Loudons had recognized the situation and left the leadership up to him. . . .

". . . years that the crops failed. Years of storms, or floods. Troubles with those beast-men in the woods.

"And you were alone, as we were, with no one to help.

"We want to put all men who are still men in touch with one another, so that they can help each other in trouble, and work together.

"If this isn't done, everything that makes men different from beasts will soon be no more."

"He's right. One of us, alone, is helpless," the Reader said. "It is only in the Toon that there is strength. He wants to organize a Toon of all Toons."

"That's about it. We are beginning to make helicopters, like the one Loudons and I came in. We'll furnish your community with one or more of them. We can give you a radio, so that you can communicate with other communities. We can give you rifles and machine guns and ammunition, to fight the – the Scowrers, did you call them? And we can give you atomic engines, so that you can build machines for yourselves."

"Some of our people, – Alex Barrett here, the gunsmith, and Stan Markovitch, the distiller, and Harrison Grant, the ironworker – get their living by making things. How'd they make out, after your machines came in here?" Verner Hughes asked.

"We've thought of that. We had that problem with other groups we've helped," Loudons said. "In some communities, everybody owns everything in common and so we don't have much of a problem. Is that the way you do it, here?"

"Well, no. If a man makes a thing, or digs it out of the ruins, or catches it in the woods, it's his."

"Then we'll work out some way. Give the machines to the people who are already in a trade, or something like that. We'll have to talk it over with you and with the people concerned."

"How is it you took so long finding us?" Alex Barrett asked. "It's been two hundred or so years since the Wars."

"Alex! You see but you do not observe!" The Toon Leader rebuked. "These people have their flying machines, which are highly complicated mechanisms. They would have to make tools and machines to make them, and tools and machines to make those tools and machines. They would have to find materials, often going in search of them. The marvel is not that they took so long, but that they did it so quickly."

"That's right," Altamont said. "Originally, Fort Ridgeway was a military research and development center. As the country became disorganized, the Government set this project up to develop ways of improvising power and transportation and communication methods and extracting raw materials. If they'd had a little more time, they might have saved the country.

"As it was, they were able to keep themselves alive, and keep something like civilization going at the Fort, while the whole country was breaking apart around them.

"Then, when the rockets stopped falling, they started to rebuild. Fortunately, more than half the technicians at the Fort were women, so there was no question of them dying out.

"But it's only been in the last twenty years that we've been able to make nuclear-electric engines, and this is the first time any of us have gotten east of the Mississippi."

"How did your group manage to survive?" Loudons asked. "You call it the Toon. I suppose that's what the word platoon has become, with time. You were, originally, a military platoon?"

"*Pla*-toon!" the white-bearded man said. "Of all the unpardonable stupidities! Of course that's what it was. And the title, Tenant, was originally lieu-tenant. I know that, though we have dropped all use of the first part of the word. But that should have led me, if I had used my wits, to deduce platoon from toon."

The Tenant shook his head in dismay at his stupidity and Loudons found himself forced to say, "One syllable like that could have come from many words."

IV

The Tenant smiled at Loudons and said, "Your courtesy does not excuse our stupidity. We know our history and we should have identified the word accurately.

"Yes, we were originally a . . . a *pla*-toon of soldiers, two hundred years ago, at the time when the Wars ended. The old Toon, and the First Tenant, were guarding POWs, and there, sir," – to Loudons – "is a word we cannot trace. We have no idea what they were. In any event, the pows were all killed by a big bomb, and the First Tenant, Lieutenant Gilbert Dunbar, took his platoon and started to march to DeeCee, where the government was.

"But there was no government anymore.

"They fought with people along the way. When they needed food, or ammunition, or animals to pull their wagons, they took them, and killed those who tried to prevent them. Other people joined the toon, and when they found women they wanted, they took them.

"They did all sorts of things that would have been crimes if there had been any law, but since there was no law, it was obvious that they could be no crime.

"The First Ten – Lieutenant – kept his men together, because he had The Books. Each evening, at the end of each day's march, he read to his men out of them."

Altamont knew without looking at his associate that Loudons would be inconspicuously jotting down notes. The last was an item the sociologist would be sure to record: the white-bearded Tenant had pronounced that reference to a written testament in capital letters.

The story was continuing. . . .

". . . finally, they came here. There had been a town here, but it had been burned and destroyed, and there were people camping in the ruins.

"Some of them fought and were killed, others came in and joined the platoon.

"At first, they built shelters around this building and made this their fort. Then they cleared away the ruins, and built new houses. When the cartridges for the rifles began to get scarce, they began to make gunpowder, and new rifles, like these we are using now, to shoot without cartridges.

"Lieutenant Dunbar did this out of his own knowledge because there is nothing in The Books about making gunpowder. The guns in The Books are rifles and shotguns and revolvers and airguns. Except for the airguns, which we haven't been able to make, these all shot cartridges.

"As with your people, we did not die out because we too had women. Neither did we increase greatly – too many died or were killed young. But several times we've had to tear down the wall and rebuild it, to make room inside for more houses. And we've been clearing out a little more land for the fields each year.

"We still read and follow the teachings of The Books: we have made laws for ourselves out of them."

There was a silence during which Altamont felt himself to be the focus of attention; not obtrusively, but, nonetheless, insistently. However, this was Loudon's field and Altamont preferred not to speak.

"And we are waiting for the Slain and Risen One," Tenant Jones added, and there was no doubt that he was looking at Altamont intently. "It is impossible that He will not, sooner or later, deduce the existence of this community, if He has not done so already."

Again the silence and lack of movement, broken by Loudons this time, when he picked up the candle to re-lit his cigar. Mentally, Altamont thanked his partner.

"Well, sir," the Toon Leader changed the subject abruptly, "enough of this talk about the past. If I understand rightly, it is the future in which you gentlemen are interested." He pushed back the cuff of his hunting shirt and looked at an old and worn wrist watch. "Eleven hundred: we'll have lunch shortly.

"This afternoon, you will meet the other people of the Toon, and this evening, at eighteen hundred, we'll have a mess together. Then, when we have everyone together, we can talk over your offer to help us, and decide what it is that you can give us that we can use."

"You spoke, a while ago, of what you could do for us, in return," Altamont said. He knew that now he would have to be the one to stress their original mission: Loudons would probably be so fascinated by this society that the sociologist might never remember the primary reason for coming to Pittsburgh.

"There's one thing you can do, no further away than tomorrow, if you're willing."

He had no time to wonder at the interchange of glances around the table before the Toon Leader said, "And that is – ?"

"In Pittsburgh, somewhere, there is an underground crypt, full of books. Not printed and bound books, but spools of microfilm. Do you know what that is?"

The men of the Toon shook their heads. Altamont continued:

"They are spools on which strips of films are wound and on which pictures have been taken of books, page by page. We can make other, larger pictures from them, big enough to be read –"

"Oh, photographs, which you can enlarge. I can understand that. You mean, you can make many copies of them?"

"That's right. And you shall have copies, as soon as we can take the originals back to Fort Ridgeway, where we have the equipment for enlarging them. But while we have information which will help us to find the crypt where the books are, we will need help in getting it open."

"Of course! This is wonderful. Copies of The Books!" the Reader exclaimed. "We thought that we had the only one left in the world!"

"Not just The Books, Stamford, *other* books," the Toon Leader told him. "The books mentioned in The Books. But of course we will help you. You have a map to show where they are?"

"Not a map, just some information. But we can work out the location of the crypt."

"A ritual," Stamford Rawson said happily. "Of course!"

V

They lunched together at the house of Toon Sarge Hughes with the Toon Leader and the Reader and five or six of the leaders of the community. The food was plentiful, but Altamont found himself wishing that the first book they found in the Carnegie Library crypt would be a cook-book.

In the afternoon, he and Loudons separated.

Loudons attached himself to the Tenant, the Reader and an old woman, Irene Klein, who was almost a hundred years old and was the repository and arbiter of most of the community's oral legends.

Altamont, on the other hand, started with Alex Barrett, the gunsmith, and Mordecai Ricci, the miller, to inspect the gunshop and the grist mill. They were later joined by a half dozen more of the village craftsmen and so also visited the forge and foundry, the sawmill and the wagon shop. Altamont additionally looked at the flume, a rough structure of logs lined with sheet aluminum; and at the nitriary, a shed-roofed pit in which potassium nitrate was extracted from the community's animal refuse.

But he reversed matters when it came to visiting the powder mill on the island: he became the host and took them by helicopter to the island and then for a trip up the river.

The guests were a badly-scared lot, for the first few minutes, as they watched the ground receding under them through the transparent plastic nose. Then, when nothing serious seemed to be happening, exhilaration took the place of fear. By the time they set down on the tip of the island, the eight men were confirmed aviation enthusiasts.

The trip up-river was an even bigger success, the high point coming when Altamont set his controls for *Hover,* pointed out a snarl of driftwood in the stream, and allowed his passengers to fire one of the machine-guns at it.

The lead balls of their own black-powder rifles would have plunked into the water-logged wood without visible effect. The copper-jacketed machine-gun bullets ripped it to splinters.

They returned for a final visit to the distillery awed by what they had seen.

VI

"Monty, I don't know what the devil to make of this crowd," Loudons said, that evening, after the feast, when they had entered the helicopter and were preparing to retire.

"We've run into some weird communities – that lot down in New Mexico who live in the church and claim that they have a divine mission to redeem the world by prayer, fasting, and flagellation.

"Or those yogis in Los Angeles –"

"Or the Blackout Boys in Detroit!" Altamont interrupted. He had good reason to remember them.

"That's understandable," Loudons said, "after what their ancestors went through in the last war. And so are the others, in their own way.

"But this crowd here!" Loudons put down his cigar and began chewing on his mustache, a sure sign that he was more than puzzled: he was a very worried man.

Altamont respected his partner's abilities in this area. However, he also knew that the best way to get his friend to work any problem was to have him do it in conversation.

"What has you stopped, Jim?"

"Number of things, Monty. They're hard to explain because –" the sociologist shrugged, winced a little as the gesture pushed his leg down on the edge of his bunk – "well, let me just mention them.

"These people are the descendants of an old United States Army platoon, yet they have a fully-developed religion centered on a slain and resurrected god.

"Now, Monty, with all due respect to the old US Army, that just doesn't make sense! Normally, it would take *thousands* of years for a slain-god religion to develop, and then only in a special situation, from the field-fertility magic of primitive agriculturists.

"Well, you saw those people's fields from the air. Some members of that old platoon were men who knew the latest methods of scientific farming. They didn't need naïve fairy tales about the planting and germination of seed."

"Sure this religion isn't just a variant of Christianity?"

"Absolutely not!

"In the first place, these Sacred Books cannot be the Bible – you heard Tenant Jones say that they mentioned firearms that used cartridges. That means they can't be older than 1860 at the earliest.

"And, in the second place, this slain god wasn't crucified, or put to death by any form of execution: he perished, together with his enemy, in combat, and both god and devil were later resurrected."

Loudons picked up his cigar again. "By the way, the Enemy is supposed to be the mastermind back of these cannibal savages in the woods and also in the ruins."

"Did you get a look at these Sacred Books, or find out what they might be?"

Loudons shook his head disgustedly. "Every time I brought up the question, they evaded me. The Tenant sent the Reader out to bring in this old lady, Irene Klein – she was a perfect gold-mine of information about the history and traditions of the platoon, by the way – and then he sent the Reader out on some other errand, undoubtedly to pass the word around not to talk to us about their religion."

"I don't get that," Altamont said. "They showed me everything – their gunshop, their powder mill, their defenses, everything."

He smoked in silence for a moment, then added, in an apologetic tone, "Jim, I'm sure you've thought of this: the slain god couldn't be the original platoon commander, could he?"

"I've thought of it, and he isn't, Monty.

"No, definitely not, though they have the greatest respect for his memory – decorate his grave regularly, drink toasts to him, and so on. But he hasn't been deified. They got the idea for this god of theirs out of the Sacred Books."

Loudons put the cigar down again and returned to chewing his mustache. "Monty, this has me worried like the devil:

"I believe that they suspect that *you* are the Slain and Risen One!"

Altamont considered the idea, then nodded slowly. "Could be, at that. I know the Tenant came up to me, very respectfully, and said, 'I hope you don't think, sir, that I was presumptuous in trying to display my humble deductive abilities to *you.*'"

"What did you say?" Loudons demanded rather sharply.

"Told him certainly not, that he'd used a good, quick method of demonstrating that he and his people weren't like those mindless subhumans in the woods."

"That was all right," Loudons approved, but then his worries returned. "I don't know how we're going to handle this –"

"Jim, how about that pows business? Is there something there?"

"Monty!" Loudons voice was dryly chiding as he took a pad of paper and scribbled briefly. "Take a look and figure for yourself."

Altamont looked at the paper. Loudons had simply printed the first three letters of the word in capitals and separated each letter with a period. "Ouch! Yes, of course, that's what an infantry platoon would be guarding.

"Go ahead, Jim, this is your end of our business. I'll stay out of it and, especially, I'll keep my mouth shut."

"I don't think you'll be able to," Loudons said soberly. "As things stand now, they only suspect that you are their deity.

"And that means this: we're on trial here!"

"We have been in spots like this before, Jim," Altamont reminded his friend.

"Not like this, Monty, and let me explain.

"I get the impression here that logic, not faith, is the supreme religious virtue. And get this, Monty, because it's something practically unheard of: skepticism is a religious obligation, not a sin!

"I wish I knew. . . ."

VII

Tenant Mycroft Jones, Reader Stamford Rawson, Toon Sarge Verner Hughes, and his son, Murray Hughes, sat around the bare-topped table in the room on the second floor of the Aitch-Cue House. A lighted candle flickered in the cool breeze that came in through the open window, throwing their shadows back and forth on the walls.

"Pass the tantalus, Murray," the Tenant said, and the youngest of the four handed the corncob-corked bottle to the eldest. Tenant Jones filled his cup and then sat staring at it, while Verner Hughes thrust his pipe into the toe of the moccasin and filled it. Finally, the Tenant drank about half the clear, wild-plum brandy.

"Gentlemen, I am baffled," he confessed. "We have three alternate possibilities here and we dare not disregard any of them.

"Either this man who calls himself Altamont is truly He, or his is merely what we are asked to believe, one of a community of men like ours, with more of the old knowledge than we possess."

"You know my views," Verner Hughes said. "I cannot believe that He was more than a man, as we are. A great, a good, a wise man, but a man and mortal."

"Let's not go into that, now." The Reader emptied his cup and took the bottle, filling it again. "You know my views, too. I hold that He is no longer upon earth in the flesh, but lives in the spirit and is only with us in the spirit.

"But you said there were three possibilities, none of which can be eliminated. What was your third possibility, Tenant?"

"That they are creatures of the Enemy, perhaps that one or the other of them is the Enemy."

Reader Rawson, lifting his cup to his lips, almost strangled. The Hugheses, father and son stared at Tenant Jones in horror.

"The Enemy – with such weapons and resources!" Murray Hughes gasped. Then he emptied his cup and refilled it. "No! I can't believe that: he would have struck before this and wiped us all out!"

"Not necessarily, Murray," the Tenant replied. "Until he became convinced that his agents, the Scowrers, could do nothing against us, he would bide his time. He sits motionless, like a spider, at the center of the web; he does little himself; his agents are numerous.

"Or, perhaps, he wishes to recruit us into this hellish organization."

"It is a possibility," the Reader admitted, "and one which we can neither accept or reject safely. And we must learn the truth as soon as possible. If this man is really He, we must not spurn Him on mere suspicion. If he is a man, come to help us, we must accept his help; if he is speaking the truth, the people who sent him could do wonders for us, and the greatest wonder would be to make us again a part of a civilized community.

"And if he is the Enemy. . . ." Rawson left the sentence unfinished, but his face was grim.

"But if he is really He," Murray said, a little diffidently, for he was not yet accustomed to being included in the council of the elders, "I think we are on trial."

"What do you mean, son? Oh, I see. Of course, I don't believe that he is, but that's mere doubt, not negative certainty. However, if I'm wrong, if this man is truly He, we are worthy of him, we will penetrate his disguise."

"A very pretty problem, gentlemen," the Tenant said, smacking his lips over his brandy, "for all that it may be a deadly serious one for us. There is, of course, nothing we can do tonight. But, tomorrow, we have promised to help our visitors, whoever they may be, in searching for this crypt in the city.

"Murray, you were to be in charge of the detail that was to accompany them. Carry on as arranged, and say nothing of our suspicions, but advise your men to keep a sharp watch on the strangers, that they may learn all they can from them.

"Stamford, you and Verner and I will go along. We should, if we have any wits at all, observe something."

VIII

"Listen to this infernal thing!" Altamont raged. "'Wielding a gold-plated spade handled with oak from an original rafter of the Congressional Library, at three-fifteen one afternoon last week—' One afternoon last week!" He cursed luridly. "Why couldn't that blasted magazine say what afternoon? I've gone over a lot of twentieth century copies of that magazine and that expression was a regular cliché with them."

Loudons looked over his shoulder at the photostated magazine page.

"Well, we know it was between June thirteen and nineteen, inclusive," he said. "And there's a picture of the university president, complete with gold-plated spade, breaking ground. Call it Wednesday, the sixteenth. Over there's the tip of the shadow of the old Cathedral of Learning, about a hundred yards away. There are so many inexactitudes, that one'll probably cancel out the other."

"That's so, and it's also pretty futile getting angry at somebody who's been dead two hundred years, but why couldn't they say Wednesday, or Monday, or Saturday, or whatever?"

Monty checked back in the astronomical handbook, and the photostated pages of the old almanac, then looked over his calculations. "All right, here is the angle of the shadow, and the compass-bearing.

"I had a look, yesterday, when I was taking the local citizenry on that junket. The old baseball diamond at Forbes Field is plainly visible, and I located the ruins of the Cathedral of Learning from that.

"Here's the above-sea level altitude of the top of the tower. After you've landed us, go up to this altitude – use the barometric altimeter, not the radar – and hold position."

Loudons leaned forward from the desk to the contraption Altamont had rigged up in the nose of the helicopter; one of the telescope-sighted hunting rifles clamped in a vise, with a compass and a spirit-level under it.

"Rifle's pointing downward at the correct angle now?" he asked. "Good. Then all I have to do is to hold the helicopter steady, keep it at the right altitude, level and pointed in the right direction, and watch through the sight while you move the flag around, and direct you by radio."

"Simple, if I had been born quintuplets!"

"Mr. Altamont! Doctor Loudons!" a voice outside the helicopter called. "Are you ready for us now?"

Altamont went to the open door and looked out. The old Toon Leader, the Reader, Toon Sarge Hughes, his son and four young men in buckskins with slung rifles were standing outside.

"I have decided," the Tenant said, "that Mr. Rawson and Sarge Hughes and I would be of more help than an equal number of young men. We may not be as active, but we do know the old ruins better, especially the paths and hiding places of the Scowrers. These four young men you probably met last evening, but it will do no harm to introduce them again.

"Birdy Edwards; Sholto Jiminez; Jefferson Burns; Murdo Olsen."

"Very pleased, Tenant, gentlemen. I met all of you young men last evening and I remember you," Altamont said. "Now, if you'll crowd in here, I'll explain what we're going to try to do."

He showed them the old picture. "You see where the shadow of a tall building falls?" he asked. "We know the height and location of this building. Doctor Loudons will hold this helicopter at exactly the position of the top of the building and aim through the sights of the rifle, there. One of you will have this flag in his hand, and will move it back and forth. Doctor Loudons will tell us when the flag is in sight of the rifle."

"He'll need a good pair of lungs to do that," Verner Hughes commented.

"We'll use the radio. A portable set on the ground, and the helicopter's radio set," Altamont said.

To his surprise, he was met with looks of incomprehension. He had not supposed that these people would have lost all memory of radio communication.

"Why, that's wonderful!" the Reader exclaimed, when the explanation was concluded. "You can talk directly. How much better than just sending a telegram!"

"But, finding the crypt by the shadow, that's exactly like the –" Murray Hughes began, then stopped short. Immediately, he began talking about the rifle that was to be used as a surveying transit, comparing it with the ones in the big first-floor room at the Aitch-Cue House.

Locating the point where the shadow of the old Cathedral of Learning had fallen proved easier than either Altamont or Loudons had expected. The towering building was now a tumbled mass of slagged rubble, but it was quite possible to determine its original center, and with the old data from the excellent reference library at Fort Ridgeway, its height above sea level was known. After a little jockeying, the helicopter came to a hovering stop, and the slanting barrel of the rifle in the vise pointed downward along the line of the shadow that had been cast on that afternoon in June, 1993.

The cross-hairs of the scope sight centered almost exactly on the spot Altamont had estimated on the map.

Guiding himself by peering through the rifle-sight, Loudons brought the helicopter slanting down to land on the sheet of fused glass that had once been a grassy campus.

"Well, this is probably it," Altamont said. "We didn't have to bother fussing around with that flag after all. That hump over there looks as though it had been a small building, and there's nothing corresponding to it on the city map. That may be the bunker over the stair-head to the crypt."

They began unloading equipment – a small, portable nuclear-electric conversion unit, a powerful solenoid-hammer, crowbars and entrenching tools, tins of blasting plastic. They took out the two hunting rifles and the auto-carbines, and Altamont showed the young men of Murray Hughes' detail how to use them.

"If you will pardon me, sir," the Tenant said to Altamont, "I think it would be a good idea if your companion went up in the flying machine and circled over us, to keep watch for the Scowrers. There are quite a few of them, particularly farther up the rivers, to the east, where the damage was not so great and they can find cellars and shelters and buildings to live in."

"Good idea. That way, we won't have to put out guards," Altamont said. "From the looks of this, we'll need everybody to help dig into that thing. Hand out one of the portable radios, Jim and go up to about a thousand feet. If you see anything suspicious, give us a yell, then spray it with bullets, and find out what it is afterward."

They waited until the helicopter had climbed to position and was circling above, and then turned their attention to the place where the sheet of fused earth and stone bulged upward. It must have been almost ground-zero of one of the hydrogen-bombs: the wreckage of the Cathedral of Learning had fallen predominantly to the north, and the Carnegie Library was tumbled to the east.

"I think the entrance would be on this side, toward the Library," Altamont said. "Let's try it, to begin with."

He used the solenoid-hammer, slowly pounding a hole in the glaze, and placed a small charge of the plastic explosive. Chunks of the lavalike stuff pelted down between the little mound and the huge one of the old library, blowing a hole six feet in diameter and the two and a half feet deep, revealing concrete bonded with crushed steel-mill slag.

"We missed the door," Altamont said. "That means we'll have to tunnel in through who knows how much concrete. Well. . . ."

He used a second and larger charge, after digging a hole a foot deep. When he and his helpers came up to look, they found a large mass of concrete blown out, and solid steel behind it. Altamont cut two more holes, one on either side of the blown-out place, and fired a charge in each of them, bringing down more concrete.

He found he hadn't missed the door after all. It had merely been concreted over.

A few more shots cleared it, and after some work, they got it open. There was a room inside, concrete-floored and entirely empty. Altamont stood in the doorway and inspected the interior with his flashlight; he heard somebody behind him say something about a most peculiar sort of dark-lantern.

Across the small room, on the opposite wall, was a bronze plaque.

The plaque carried quite a lengthy inscription, including the names of all the persons and institutions participating in the microfilm project. The History Department at the Fort would be interested in that, but the only thing that interested Altamont was the statement that the floor had been laid over the trapdoor leading to the vault where the microfilms were stored. He went outside to the radio.

"Hello, Jim. We're inside, but the films were stored in an underground vault, and so we have to tear up a concrete floor," he said. "Go back to the village and gather up all the men you can carry. I don't want to use explosives inside. The interior of the crypt oughtn't to be damaged. Besides, I don't know what a blast in there might do to the film, and I don't want to take any chances."

"No, of course not. How thick do you think the floor is?"

"Haven't the least idea. Plenty thick, I would guess. Those films would have to be well-buried, to shield them from radioactivity. We can expect that it will take some time."

"All right. I'll be back as soon as I can."

The helicopter turned and went windmilling away, over what had been the Golden Triangle, down the Ohio. Altamont went back to the little concrete bunker and sat down, lighting his pipe. Murray Hughes and his four riflemen spread out, one circling around the glazed butte that had been the Cathedral of Learning, another climbing to the top of the old Library, and the others taking positions to the south and east.

Altamont sat in silence, smoking his pipe and trying to form some conception of the wealth under that concrete floor.

It was no use.

Jim Loudons probably understood a little more clearly what those books would mean to the world of today, and what they could do toward shaping the world of the future.

There was a library at Fort Ridgeway, and it was an excellent one . . . for its purpose. In 1996, when the rockets had come crashing down, it had contained the cream of the world's technical knowledge – and very little else. There was only a little fiction, a few books of ideas, just enough to give the survivors a tantalizing glimpse of the world of their fathers.

But now. . . .

A rifle banged to the south and east, and banged again. Either Murray Hughes or Birdy Edwards: it was one of the two hunting rifles from the helicopter.

On the heels of the reports, they heard a voice shouting, "Scowrers! A lot of them, coming from up the river!"

A moment later, there was a light whip-crack of one of the muzzle-loaders, from the top of the old Carnegie Library, and Altamont could see a wisp of grey-white smoke drifting away from where it had been fired.

Altamont jumped to his feet and raced for the radio, picking it up and bring it to the bunker.

Tenant Jones, old Reader Rawson, and Verner Hughes had caught up their rifles. The Tenant was shouting. "Come on in! Everybody, come on in!"

The boy on top of the library began scrambling down. Another came running from the direction of the half-demolished Cathedral of Learning, a third from the baseball field that had served as Altamont's point of reference the afternoon before.

The fourth, Murray Hughes, was running in from the ruins of the old Carnegie Tech buildings, and Birdy Edwards sped up the main road from Schenley Park. Once, twice, as he ran, Murray Hughes paused, turned, and fired behind him.

Then his pursuers came into sight!

They ran erect, they wore a few rags of skin garments, and they carried spears and hatchets and clubs, so they were probably classifiable as men. But their hair was long and unkempt, and their bodies were almost black with dirt and from the sun. A few of them were yelling, but most of them ran silently. They ran more swiftly than the boy they were pursuing: the distance between them narrowed every moment. There were at least fifty of them.

Verner Hughes' rifle barked, one of them dropped. As coolly as though he were shooting squirrels instead of his son's pursuers, he dropped the butt of the rifle to the ground, poured a charge of powder, patched a ball and rammed it home, replaced the ramrod. Tenant Jones fired then, and Birdy Edwards joined them, beginning to shoot with the telescope-sighted rifle.

The young man who had been north of the Cathedral of Learning had one of the auto-carbines; luckily, Altamont had providently set the control for semi-auto before giving it to him. He dropped to one knee and began to empty the clip, shooting slowly and deliberately, picking off the runners who were in the lead.

The boy who had started to climb down off the Library halted, fired his flintlock, and began reloading it.

Altamont, sitting down and propping his elbows on his knees, took both hands to the automatic which was his only weapon, emptying the magazine and replacing it. The last three savages he shot in the back: they had had enough and were running for their lives.

So far, everybody was safe. The boy in the Library came down through a place where the wall had fallen. Murray Hughes stopped running and came slowly toward the bunker, putting a fresh clip into his rifle. The others came drifting in.

"Altamont, calling Loudons," the scientist from Fort Ridgeway was saying into the radio. "Monty to Jim: can you hear me?"

Silence.

"We'd better get ready for another attack," Birdy Edwards said. "There's another gang coming from down that way. I never saw so many Scowrers!"

"Maybe there's a reason, Birdy," Tenant Jones said. "The Enemy is after big game, this time."

"Jim, where the devil are you?" Altamont fairly yelled into the radio; and as he did, he knew the answer. Loudons was in the village, away from the helicopter, gathering tools and workers.

Nothing to do but keep on trying!

"Here they come!" Reader Rawson warned.

"How far can these rifles be depended on?" Birdy Edwards wanted to know.

Altamont straightened, saw the second band of savages approaching about four hundred yards away.

"Start shooting now," he said. "Aim for the upper part of their bodies."

The two auto-loading rifles began to crack. After the first few shots, the savages took cover. Evidently they understood the capabilities and limitations of the villagers' flintlocks, but this was a terrifying surprise to them.

"Jim!" – Altamont was almost praying into the radio – "Come in, Jim!"

"What is it, Monty? I was outside."

Altamont told him.

"Those fellows you had up with you yesterday, think they could be trusted to handle the guns? A couple of them are here with me," Loudons inquired.

"Take a chance on it! It won't cost anything but my life, and that's not worth much at the present."

"All right, hold on. We'll be there in a few minutes."

"Loudons is bringing the helicopter," Altamont told the others. "All we have to do is to hold on, here, until he comes."

A naked savage raised his head from behind what might, two hundred years ago, have been a cement park-bench and he was only a hundred yards away. Reader Rawson promptly killed him and began reloading.

"I think you're right, Tenant," he said. "The Scowrers have never attacked in bands like this before. They must have a powerful reason and I can think of only one."

"That's what I'm beginning to think, too," Verner Hughes agreed. "At least, we've eliminated the third of your possibilities, Tenant. And I think probably the second, as well."

Altamont wondered what they were double-talking about. There wasn't any particular mystery about the mass attack of the wild men to him.

Debased as they were, they still possessed speech and the ability to transmit experiences. No matter how beclouded in superstition, they still remembered that aircraft dropped bombs, and bombs killed people, and where people had been killed, they would find fresh meat. They had seen the helicopter circling about, and had heard the blasting: everyone in the area had been drawn to the scene as soon as Loudons had gone down the river.

But they seemed to have forgotten that aircraft carried guns, although they did spring to their feet and start to run at the return of the helicopter.

However, most of them did not run far.

IX

Altamont and Loudons shook hands many times in front of the Aitch-Cue House, and listened to many good wishes, and repeated their promise to return. Most of the microfilmed books were to be stored in the old church. They were taking with them only the catalogue and a few of the most important works. Finally, they entered the helicopter. The crowd shouted farewell as they rose.

Altamont, at the controls, waited until they had gained five thousand feet, then turned on a compass-course for Colony Three.

"I can't wait until we're in radio range of the Fort, Jim. This is one report that I really want to make," he said.

"Of all the wonderful luck!" he went on. "And I don't know which is the more important: finding those books, or finding those people. In a few years, when we can get them supplied with modern equipment and instructed in its use –

"What's the matter, Jim? You should be even more excited than I am."

"I'm not very happy about this, Monty," Loudons confessed. "I keep thinking about what's going to happen to them."

"Why, nothing's going to happen to them. They're going to be given the means of producing more food, keeping more of them alive, giving them more leisure to develop themselves in –"

"Monty, I saw the Sacred Books."

"The deuce! What were they?"

"It. One volume. A collection of works. We have it at the Fort and I've read it. How I ever missed all those clues –"

"You see, Monty, what I'm worried about is what's going to happen to those people when they find out that we're not really Sherlock Holmes and Doctor Watson. . . ."

THE END

Rebel Raider

It was almost midnight, on January 2, 1863, and the impromptu party at the Ratcliffe home was breaking up. The guest of honor, General J. E. B. Stuart, felt that he was overstaying his welcome – not at the Ratcliffe home, where everybody was soundly Confederate, but in Fairfax County, then occupied by the Union Army.

About a week before, he had come raiding up from Culpepper with a strong force of cavalry, to spend a merry Christmas in northern Virginia and give the enemy a busy if somewhat less than happy New Year's. He had shot up outposts, run off horses from remount stations, plundered supply depots, burned stores of forage; now, before returning to the main Confederate Army, he had paused to visit his friend Laura Ratcliffe. And, of course, there had been a party. There was always a party when Jeb Stuart was in any one place long enough to organize one.

They were all crowding into the hallway – the officers of Stuart's staff, receiving their hats and cloaks from the servants and buckling on their weapons; the young ladies, their gay dresses showing only the first traces of wartime shabbiness; the matrons who chaperoned them; Stuart himself, the center of attention, with his hostess on his arm.

"It's a shame you can't stay longer, General," Laura Ratcliffe was saying. "It's hard on us, living in conquered territory, under enemy rule."

"Well, I won't desert you entirely, Miss Ratcliffe," Stuart told her. "I'm returning to Culpepper in the morning, as you know, but I mean to leave Captain Mosby behind with a few men, to look after the loyal Confederate people here until we can return in force and in victory."

Hearing his name, one of the men in grey turned, his hands raised to hook the fastening at the throat of his cloak. Just four days short of his thirtieth birthday, he looked even more youthful; he was considerably below average height, and so slender as to give the impression of frailness. His hair and the beard he was wearing at the time were very light brown. He wore an officer's uniform without insignia of rank, and instead of a saber he carried a pair of 1860-model Colt .44's on his belt, with the butts to the front so that either revolver could be drawn with either hand, backhand or crossbody.

There was more than a touch of the dandy about him. The cloak he was fastening was lined with scarlet silk and the grey cock-brimmed hat the slave was holding for him was plumed with a squirrel tail. At first glance he seemed no more than one of the many young gentlemen of the planter class serving in the Confederate cavalry. But then one looked into his eyes and got the illusion of being covered by a pair of blued pistol muzzles. He had an aura of combined ruthlessness, self confidence, good humor and impudent audacity.

For an instant he stood looking inquiringly at the general. Then he realized what Stuart had said, and the blue eyes sparkled. This was the thing he had almost given up hoping for – an independent command and a chance to operate in the enemy's rear.

In 1855, John Singleton Mosby, newly graduated from the University of Virginia, had opened a law office at Bristol, Washington County, Virginia, and a year later he had married.

The son of a well-to-do farmer and slave-owner, his boyhood had been devoted to outdoor sports, especially hunting, and he was accounted an expert horseman and a dead shot, even in a society in which skill with guns and horses was taken for granted. Otherwise, the outbreak of the war had found him without military qualifications and completely uninterested in military matters. Moreover, he had been a rabid anti-secessionist.

It must be remembered, however, that, like most Southerners, he regarded secession as an entirely local issue, to be settled by the people of each state for themselves. He took no exception to the position that a state had the constitutional right to sever its connection with the Union if its people so desired. His objection to secession was based upon what he considered to be political logic. He realized that, once begun, secession was a process which could only end in reducing America to a cluster of impotent petty sovereignties, torn by hostilities, incapable of any concerted action, a fair prey to any outside aggressor.

However, he was also a believer in the paramount sovereignty of the states. He was first of all a Virginian. So, when Virginia voted in favor of secession, Mosby, while he deplored the choice, felt that he had no alternative but to accept it. He promptly enlisted in a locally organized cavalry company, the Washington Mounted Rifles, under a former U. S. officer and West Point graduate, William E. Jones.

His letters to his wife told of his early military experiences – his pleasure at receiving one of the fine new Sharps carbines which Captain Jones had wangled for his company, and, later, a Colt .44 revolver: his first taste of fire in the Shenandoah Valley, where the company, now incorporated into Colonel Stuart's First Virginia Cavalry, were covering Johnston's march to re-enforce Beauregard: his rather passive participation in the big battle at Manassas. He was keenly disappointed at being held in reserve throughout the fighting. Long afterward, it was to be his expressed opinion that the Confederacy had lost the war by failing to follow the initial victory and exploit the rout of McDowell's army.

The remainder of 1861 saw him doing picket duty in Fairfax County. When Stuart was promoted to brigadier general, and Captain Jones took his place as colonel of the First Virginia, Mosby became the latter's adjutant. There should have been a commission along with this post, but this seems to have been snarled in red tape at Richmond and never came through. It was about this time that Mosby first came to Stuart's personal attention. Mosby spent a night at headquarters after escorting a couple of young ladies who had been living outside the Confederate lines and were anxious to reach relatives living farther south.

Stuart had been quite favorably impressed with Mosby, and when, some time later, the latter lost his place as adjutant of the First by reason of Jones' promotion to brigadier general and Fitzhugh Lee's taking over the regiment, Mosby became one of Stuart's headquarters scouts.

Scouting for Jeb Stuart was not the easiest work in the world, nor the safest, but Mosby appears to have enjoyed it, and certainly made good at it. It was he who scouted the route for Stuart's celebrated "Ride Around MacClellan" in June, 1862, an exploit which brought his name to the favorable attention of General Lee. By this time, still without commission, he was accepted at Stuart's headquarters as a sort of courtesy officer, and generally addressed as "Captain" Mosby. Stuart made several efforts to get him commissioned, but War Department red tape seems to have blocked all of them. By this time, too, Mosby had become convinced of the utter worthlessness of the saber as a cavalryman's weapon, and for his own armament adopted a pair of Colts.

The revolver of the Civil War was, of course, a percussion-cap weapon. Even with the powder and bullet contained in a combustible paper cartridge, loading such an arm was a slow process: each bullet had to be forced in the front of the chamber on top of its propellant charge by means of a hinged rammer under the barrel, and a tiny copper cap had to be placed on each nipple. It was nothing to attempt on a prancing horse. The Union cavalryman was armed with a single-shot carbine – the seven-shot Spencer repeater was not to make its battlefield appearance until late in 1863 – and one revolver, giving him a total of seven shots without reloading. With a pair of six-shooters, Mosby had a five-shot advantage over any opponent he was likely to encounter. As he saw it, tactical strength lay in the number of shots which could be delivered without reloading, rather than in the number of men firing them. Once he reached a position of independent command, he was to adhere consistently to this principle.

On July 14, 1862, General John Pope, who had taken over a newly created Union Army made up of the commands of McDowell, Banks and Fremont, issued a bombastic and tactless order to his new command, making invidious comparisons between the armies in the west and those in the east. He said, "I hear constantly of 'taking strong positions and holding them,' of 'lines of retreat,' and of 'bases of supplies.' Let us discard all such ideas. Let us study the probable lines of retreat of our opponents, and leave our own to take care of themselves."

That intrigued Mosby. If General Pope wasn't going to take care of his own rear, somebody ought to do it for him, and who better than John Mosby? He went promptly to Stuart, pointing out Pope's disinterest in his own lines of supply and communication, and asked that he be given about twenty men and detailed to get into Pope's rear and see what sort of disturbance he could create.

Stuart doubted the propriety of sending men into what was then Stonewall Jackson's territory, but he gave Mosby a letter to Jackson, recommending the bearer highly and outlining what he proposed doing, with the request that he be given some men to try it. With this letter, Mosby set out for Jackson's headquarters.

He never reached his destination. On the way, he was taken prisoner by a raiding force of New York cavalry, and arrived, instead, at Old Capitol jail in Washington. Stuart requested his exchange at once, and Mosby spent only about ten days in Old Capitol, and then was sent down the Potomac on an exchange boat, along with a number of other prisoners of war, for Hampton Roads.

The boat-load of prisoners, about to be exchanged and returned to their own army, were allowed to pass through a busy port of military embarkation and debarkation, with every opportunity to observe everything that was going on, and, to make a bad matter worse, the steamboat captain was himself a Confederate sympathizer. So when Mosby, from the exchange boat, observed a number of transports lying at anchor, he had no trouble at all in learning that they carried Burnside's men, newly brought north from the Carolinas. With the help of the steamboat captain, Mosby was able to learn that the transports were bound for Acquia Creek, on the Potomac; that meant that the re-enforcements were for Pope.

As soon as he was exchanged, Mosby made all haste for Lee's headquarters to report what he had discovered. Lee, remembering Mosby as the man who had scouted ahead of Stuart's Ride Around MacClellan, knew that he had a hot bit of information from a credible source. A dispatch rider was started off at once for Jackson, and Jackson struck Pope at Cedar Mountain before he could be re-enforced. Mosby returned to Stuart's headquarters, losing no time in promoting a pair of .44's to replace the ones lost when captured, and found his stock with Stuart at an all-time high as a result of his recent feat of espionage while in the hands of the enemy.

So he was with Stuart when Stuart stopped at Laura Ratcliffe's home, and was on hand when Stuart wanted to make one of his characteristic gestures of gallantry. And so he finally got his independent command – all of six men – and orders to operate in the enemy's rear.

Whatever Stuart might have had in mind in leaving him behind "to look after the loyal Confederate people," John Mosby had no intention of posting himself in Laura Ratcliffe's front yard as a guard of honor. He had a theory of guerrilla warfare which he wanted to test. In part, it derived from his experiences in the Shenandoah Valley and in Fairfax County, but in larger part, it was based upon his own understanding of the fundamental nature of war.

The majority of guerrilla leaders have always been severely tactical in their thinking. That is to say, they have been concerned almost exclusively with immediate results. A troop column is ambushed, a picket post attacked, or a supply dump destroyed for the sake of the immediate loss of personnel or materiel so inflicted upon the enemy. Mosby, however, had a well-conceived strategic theory. He knew, in view of the magnitude of the war, that the tactical effects of his operations would simply be lost in the overall picture. But, if he could create enough uproar in the Union rear, he believed that he could force the withdrawal from the front of a regiment or even a brigade to guard against his attacks and, in some future battle, the absence of that regiment or brigade might tip the scale of battle or, at least, make some future Confederate victory more complete or some defeat less crushing.

As soon as Stuart's column started southward, Mosby took his six men across Bull Run Mountain to Middleburg, where he ordered them to scatter out, billet themselves at outlying farms, and meet him at the Middleburg hotel on the night of January 10. Meanwhile he returned alone to Fairfax County, spending the next week making contacts with the people and gathering information.

On the night of Saturday, January 10, he took his men through the gap at Aldie and into Fairfax County. His first stop was at a farmhouse near Herndon Station, where he had friends, and there he met a woodsman, trapper and market hunter named John Underwood, who, with his two brothers, had been carrying on a private resistance movement against the Union occupation ever since the Confederate Army had moved out of the region. Overjoyed at the presence of regular Confederate troops, even as few as a half-dozen, Underwood offered to guide Mosby to a nearby Union picket post.

Capturing this post was no particularly spectacular feat of arms. Mosby's party dismounted about 200 yards away from it and crept up on it, to find seven members of the Fifth New York squatting around a fire, smoking, drinking coffee and trying to keep warm. Their first intimation of the presence of any enemy nearer than the Rappahannock River came when Mosby and his men sprang to their feet, leveled revolvers and demanded their surrender. One cavalryman made a grab for his carbine and Mosby shot him; the others put up their hands. The wounded man was given first aid, wrapped in a blanket and placed beside the fire to wait until the post would be relieved. The others were mounted on their own horses and taken to Middleburg, where they were paroled i.e., released after they gave their word not to take up arms again against the Confederacy. This not entirely satisfactory handling of prisoners was the only means left open to Mosby with his small force, behind enemy lines.

The next night, Mosby stayed out of Fairfax County to allow the excitement to die down a little, but the night after, he and his men, accompanied by Underwood, raided a post where the Little River Turnpike crossed Cub Run. Then, after picking up a two-man road patrol en route, they raided another post near Fryingpan Church. This time they brought back fourteen prisoners and horses.

In all, he and his sextet had captured nineteen prisoners and twenty horses. But Mosby still wasn't satisfied. What he wanted was a few more men and orders to operate behind the Union army on a permanent basis. So, after paroling the catch of the night before, he told John Underwood to get busy gathering information and establishing contacts, and he took his six men back to Culpepper, reporting his activities to Stuart and claiming that under his existing orders he had not felt justified in staying away from the army longer. At the same time, he asked for a larger detail and orders to continue operating in northern Virginia.

In doing so, he knew he was taking a chance that Stuart would keep him at Culpepper, but as both armies had gone into winter quarters after Fredericksburg with only a minimum of outpost activity, he reasoned that Stuart would be willing to send him back. As it happened, Stuart was so delighted with the success of Mosby's brief activity that he gave him fifteen men, all from the First Virginia Cavalry, and orders to operate until recalled. On January 18, Mosby was back at Middleburg, ready to go to work in earnest.

As before, he scattered his men over the countryside, quartering them on the people. This time, before scattering them, he told them to meet him at Zion Church, just beyond the gap at Aldie, on the night of the 28th. During the intervening ten days, he was not only busy gathering information but also in an intensive recruiting campaign among the people of upper Fauquier and lower Loudoun Counties.

In this last, his best selling-point was a recent act of the Confederate States Congress called the Scott Partisan Ranger Law. This piece of legislation was, in effect, an extension of the principles of prize law and privateering to land warfare. It authorized the formation of independent cavalry companies, to be considered part of the armed forces of the Confederacy, their members to serve without pay and mount themselves, in return for which they were to be entitled to keep any spoil of war captured from the enemy. The terms "enemy" and "spoil of war" were defined so liberally as to cover almost anything not the property of the government or citizens of the Confederacy. There were provisions, also, entitling partisan companies to draw on the Confederate government for arms and ammunition and permitting them to turn in and receive payment for any spoil which they did not wish to keep for themselves.

The law had met with considerable opposition from the Confederate military authorities, who claimed that it would attract men and horses away from the regular service and into ineffective freebooting. There is no doubt that a number of independent companies organized under the Scott Law accomplished nothing of military value. Some degenerated into mere bandit gangs, full of deserters from both sides, and terrible only to the unfortunate Confederate citizens living within their range of operations. On the other hand, as Mosby was to demonstrate, a properly employed partisan company could be of considerable use.

It was the provision about booty, however, which appealed to Mosby. As he intended operating in the Union rear, where the richest plunder could be found, he hoped that the prospect would attract numerous recruits. The countryside contained many men capable of bearing arms who had remained at home to look after their farms but who would be more than willing to ride with him now and then in hope of securing a new horse for farm work, or some needed harness, or food and blankets for their families. The regular Mosby Men called them the "Conglomerates," and Mosby himself once said that they resembled the Democrat party, being "held together only by the cohesive power of public plunder."

Mosby's first operation with his new force was in the pattern of the other two – the stealthy dismounted approach and sudden surprise of an isolated picket post. He brought back eleven prisoners and twelve horses and sets of small arms, and, as on the night of the 10th, left one wounded enemy behind. As on the previous occasions, the prisoners were taken as far as Middleburg before being released on parole.

For this reason, Mosby was sure that Colonel Sir Percy Wyndham, commander of the brigade which included the Fifth New York, Eighteenth Pennsylvania and the First Vermont, would assume that this village was the raiders' headquarters. Colonel Wyndham, a European-trained soldier, would scarcely conceive of any military force, however small, without a regular headquarters and a fixed camp. Therefore, Wyndham would come looking for him at Middleburg. So, with a companion named Fountain Beattie, Mosby put up for what remained of the night at the home of a Mr. Lorman Chancellor, on the road from Aldie a few miles east of Middleburg. The rest of the company were ordered to stay outside Middleburg.

Mosby's estimate of his opponent was uncannily accurate. The next morning, about daybreak, he and Beattie were wakened by one of the Chancellor servants and warned that a large body of Union cavalry was approaching up the road from Aldie. Peering through the window shutters, they watched about 200 men of the Fifth New York ride by, with Colonel Wyndham himself in the lead. As soon as they were out of sight up the road, Mosby and Beattie, who had hastily dressed, dashed downstairs for their horses.

"I'm going to keep an eye on these people," Mosby told Beattie. "Gather up as many men as you can, and meet me in about half an hour on the hill above Middleburg. But hurry! I'd rather have five men now than a hundred by noon."

When Beattie with six men rejoined Mosby, he found the latter sitting on a stump, munching an apple and watching the enemy through his field glasses. Wyndham, who had been searching Middleburg for "Mosby's headquarters," was just forming his men for a push on to Upperville, where he had been assured by the canny Middleburgers that Mosby had his camp.

Mosby and his men cantered down the hillside to the road as Wyndham's force moved out of the village and then broke into a mad gallop to overtake them.

It was always hard to be sure whether jackets were dirty grey or faded blue. As the Union soldier had a not unfounded belief that the Virginia woods were swarming with bushwhackers (Confederate guerillas), the haste of a few men left behind to rejoin the column was quite understandable. The rearguard pulled up and waited for them. Then, at about twenty yards' range, one of the New Yorkers, a sergeant, realized what was happening and shouted a warning:

"They're Rebs!"

Instantly one of Mosby's men, Ned Hurst, shot him dead. Other revolvers, ready drawn, banged, and several Union cavalrymen were wounded. Mosby and his followers hastily snatched the bridles of three others, disarmed them and turned, galloping away with them.

By this time, the main column, which had not halted with the rearguard, was four or five hundred yards away. There was a brief uproar, a shouting of contradictory orders, and then the whole column turned and came back at a gallop. Mosby, four of his men, and the three prisoners, got away, but Beattie and two others were captured when their horses fell on a sheet of ice treacherously hidden under the snow. There was no possibility of rescuing them. After the capture of Beattie and his companions, the pursuit stopped. Halting at a distance, Mosby saw Wyndham form his force into a compact body and move off toward Aldie at a brisk trot. He sent off the prisoners under guard of two of his men and followed Wyndham's retreat almost to Aldie without opportunity to inflict anymore damage.

During his stop at Middleburg, Wyndham had heaped coals on a growing opposition to Mosby, fostered by pro-Unionists in the neighborhood. Wyndham informed the townspeople that he would burn the town and imprison the citizens if Mosby continued the attacks on his outposts. A group of citizens, taking the threat to heart, petitioned Stuart to recall Mosby, but the general sent a stinging rebuke, telling the Middleburgers that Mosby and his men were risking their lives which were worth considerably more than a few houses and barns.

Mosby was also worried about the antipathy to the Scott Law and the partisan ranger system which was growing among some of the general officers of the Confederacy. To counteract such opposition, he needed to achieve some spectacular feat of arms which would capture the popular imagination, make a public hero of himself, and place him above criticism.

And all the while, his force was growing. The booty from his raids excited the cupidity of the more venturesome farmers, and they were exchanging the hoe for the revolver and joining him. A number of the convalescents and furloughed soldiers were arranging transfers to his command. Others, with no permanent military attachment, were drifting to Middleburg, Upperville, or Rectortown, inquiring where they might find Mosby, and making their way to join him.

There was a young Irishman, Dick Moran. There was a Fauquier County blacksmith, Billy Hibbs, who reported armed with a huge broadsword which had been the last product of his forge. There were Walter Frankland, Joe Nelson, Frank Williams and George Whitescarver, among the first to join on a permanent basis. And, one day, there was the strangest recruit of all.

A meeting was held on the 25th of February at the Blackwell farm, near Upperville, and Mosby and most of his men were in the kitchen of the farmhouse, going over a map of the section they intended raiding, when a couple of men who had been on guard outside entered, pushing a Union cavalry sergeant ahead of them.

"This Yankee says he wants to see you, Captain," one of the men announced. "He came on foot; says his horse broke a leg and had to be shot."

"Well, I'm Mosby," the guerrilla leader said. "What do you want?"

The man in blue came to attention and saluted.

"I've come here to join your company, sir," he said calmly.

There was an excited outburst from the men in the kitchen, but Mosby took the announcement in stride.

"And what's your name and unit, sergeant?"

"James F. Ames: late Fifth New York Cavalry, sir."

After further conversation, Mosby decided that the big Yankee was sincere in his avowed decision to join the forces of the Confederacy. He had some doubts about his alleged motives: the man was animated with a most vindictive hatred of the Union government, all his former officers and most of his former comrades. No one ever learned what injury, real or fancied, had driven Sergeant Ames to desertion and treason, but in a few minutes Mosby was sure that the man was through with the Union Army.

Everybody else was equally sure that he was a spy, probably sent over by Wyndham to assassinate Mosby. Eventually Mosby proposed a test of Ames' sincerity. The deserter should guide the company to a Union picket post, and should accompany the raiders unarmed: Mosby would ride behind him, ready to shoot him at the first sign of treachery. The others agreed to judge the new recruit by his conduct on the raid. A fairly strong post, at a schoolhouse at Thompson's Corners, was selected as the objective, and they set out, sixteen men beside Ames and Mosby, through a storm of rain and sleet. Stopping at a nearby farm, Mosby learned that the post had been heavily re-enforced since he had last raided it. There were now about a hundred men at the schoolhouse.

Pleased at this evidence that his campaign to force the enemy to increase his guard was bearing fruit, Mosby decided to abandon his customary tactics of dismounting at a distance and approaching on foot. On a night like this, the enemy would not be expecting him, so the raiders advanced boldly along the road, Mosby telling Ames to make whatever answer he thought would be believed in case they were challenged. However, a couple of trigger-happy vedettes let off their carbines at them, yelled, "The Rebs are coming!" and galloped for the schoolhouse.

There was nothing to do but gallop after them, and Mosby and his band came pelting in on the heels of the vedettes. Hitherto, his raids had been more or less bloodless, but this time he had a fight on his hands, and if the men in the schoolhouse had stayed inside and defended themselves with carbine fire, they would have driven off the attack. Instead, however, they rushed outside, each man trying to mount his horse. A lieutenant and seven men were killed, about twice that number wounded, and five prisoners were taken. The rest, believing themselves attacked by about twice their own strength, scattered into the woods and got away.

Ames, who had ridden unarmed, flung himself upon a Union cavalryman at the first collision and disarmed him, then threw himself into the fight with the captured saber. His conduct during the brief battle at the schoolhouse was such as to remove from everybody's mind the suspicion that his conversion to the Confederate cause was anything but genuine. Thereafter, he was accepted as a Mosby man.

He was accepted by Mosby himself as a veritable godsend, since he was acquainted with the location of every Union force in Fairfax County, and knew of a corridor by which it would be possible to penetrate Wyndham's entire system of cavalry posts as far as Fairfax Courthouse itself. Here, then, was the making of the spectacular coup which Mosby needed to answer his critics and enemies, both at Middleburg and at army headquarters. He decided to attempt nothing less than a raid upon Fairfax Courthouse, with the capture of Wyndham as its purpose.

This last would entail something of a sacrifice, for he had come to esteem Sir Percy highly as an opponent whose mind was an open book and whose every move could be predicted in advance. With Wyndham eliminated, he would have to go to the trouble of learning the mental processes of his successor.

However, Wyndham would be the ideal captive to grace a Mosby triumph, and a successful raid on Fairfax Courthouse, garrisoned as it was by between five and ten thousand Union troops, would not only secure Mosby's position in his own army but would start just the sort of a panic which would result in demands that the Union rear be re-enforced at the expense of the front.

So, on Sunday, March 8, Mosby led thirty-nine men through the gap at Aldie, the largest force that had followed him to date. It was the sort of a foul night that he liked for raiding, with a drizzling rain falling upon melting snow. It was pitch dark before they found the road between Centreville and Fairfax, along which a telegraph line had been strung to connect the main cavalry camp with General Stoughton's headquarters. Mosby sent one of his men, Harry Hatcher, up a pole to cut the wire. They cut another telegraph line at Fairfax Station and left the road, moving through the woods toward Fairfax Courthouse. At this time, only Mosby and Yank Ames knew the purpose of the expedition.

It was therefore with surprise and some consternation that the others realized where they were as they rode into the courthouse square and halted. A buzz of excited whispers rose from the men.

"That's right," Mosby assured them calmly. "We're in Fairfax Courthouse, right in the middle of ten thousand Yankees, but don't let that worry you. All but about a dozen of them are asleep. Now, if you all keep your heads and do what you're told, we'll be as safe as though we were in Jeff Davis' front parlor."

He then began giving instructions, detailing parties to round up horses and capture any soldiers they found awake and moving about. He went, himself, with several men, to the home of a citizen named Murray, where he had been told that Wyndham had quartered himself, but here he received the disappointing news that the Englishman had gone to Washington that afternoon.

A few minutes later, however, Joe Nelson came up with a prisoner, an infantryman who had just been relieved from sentry duty at General Stoughton's headquarters, who said that there had been a party there earlier in the evening and that Stoughton and several other officers were still there. Mosby, still disappointed at his failure to secure Wyndham, decided to accept Stoughton in his place. Taking several men, he went at once to the house where the prisoner said Stoughton had his headquarters.

Arriving there, he hammered loudly on the door with a revolver butt. An upstairs window opened, and a head, in a nightcap, was thrust out.

"What the devil's all the noise about?" its owner demanded. "Don't you know this is General Stoughton's headquarters?"

"I'd hoped it was; I almost killed a horse getting here," Mosby retorted. "Come down and open up; dispatches from Washington."

In a few moments, a light appeared inside on the first floor, and the door opened. A man in a nightshirt, holding a candle, stood in the doorway.

"I'm Lieutenant Prentiss, on General Stoughton's staff. The general's asleep. If you'll give me the dispatches . . ."

Mosby caught the man by the throat with his left hand and shoved a Colt into his face with his right. Dan Thomas, beside him, lifted the candle out of the other man's hand.

"And I'm Captain Mosby, General Stuart's staff. We've just taken Fairfax Courthouse. Inside, now, and take me to the general at once."

The general was in bed, lying on his face in a tangle of bedclothes. Mosby pulled the sheets off of him, lifted the tail of his nightshirt and slapped him across the bare rump.

The effect was electric. Stoughton sat up in bed, gobbling in fury. In the dim candlelight, he mistook the grey of Mosby's tunic for blue, and began a string of bloodthirsty threats of court-martial and firing squad, interspersed with oaths.

"Easy, now, General," the perpetrator of the outrage soothed. "You've heard of John Mosby, haven't you?"

"Yes; have you captured him?" In the face of such tidings, Stoughton would gladly forget the assault on his person.

Mosby shook his head, smiling seraphically. "No, General. He's captured you. I'm Mosby."

"Oh my God!" Stoughton sank back on the pillow and closed his eyes, overcome.

Knowing the precarious nature of his present advantage, Mosby then undertook to deprive Stoughton of any hope of rescue or will to resist.

"Stuart's cavalry is occupying Fairfax Courthouse," he invented, "and Stonewall Jackson's at Chantilly with his whole force. We're all moving to occupy Alexandria by morning. You'll have to hurry and dress, General."

"Is Fitzhugh Lee here?" Stoughton asked. "He's a friend of mine; we were classmates at West Point."

"Why, no; he's with Jackson at Chantilly. Do you want me to take you to him? I can do so easily if you hurry."

It does not appear that Stoughton doubted as much as one syllable of this remarkable set of prevarications. The Union Army had learned by bitter experience that Stonewall Jackson was capable of materializing almost anywhere. So he climbed out of bed, putting on his clothes.

On the way back to the courthouse square, Prentiss got away from them in the darkness, but Mosby kept a tight hold on Stoughton's bridle. By this time, the suspicion that all was not well in the county seat had begun to filter about. Men were beginning to turn out under arms all over town, and there was a confusion of challenges and replies and some occasional firing as hastily wakened soldiers mistook one another for the enemy. Mosby got his prisoners and horses together and started out of town as quickly as he could.

The withdrawal was made over much the same route as the approach, without serious incident. Thanks to the precaution of cutting the telegraph wires, the camp at Centreville knew nothing of what had happened at Fairfax Courthouse until long after the raiders were safely away. They lost all but thirty of the prisoners – in the woods outside Fairfax Courthouse, they escaped in droves – but they brought Stoughton and the two captains out safely.

The results were everything Mosby had hoped. He became a Confederate hero over night, and there was no longer any danger of his being recalled. There were several half-hearted attempts to kick him upstairs – an offer of a commission in the now defunct Virginia Provisional Army, which he rejected scornfully, and a similar offer in the regular Confederate States Army, which he politely declined because it would deprive his men of their right to booty under the Scott Law. Finally he was given a majority in the Confederate States Army, with authorization to organize a partisan battalion under the Scott Law. This he accepted, becoming Major Mosby of the Forty-Third Virginia Partisan Ranger Battalion.

The effect upon the enemy was no less satisfactory. When full particulars of the Fairfax raid reached Washington, Wyndham vanished from the picture, being assigned to other duties where less depended upon him. There was a whole epidemic of courts-martial and inquiries, some of which were still smoldering when the war ended. And Stoughton, the principal victim, found scant sympathy. President Lincoln, when told that the rebels had raided Fairfax to the tune of one general, two captains, thirty men and fifty-eight horses, remarked that he could make all the generals he wanted, but that he was sorry to lose the horses, as he couldn't make horses. As yet, there was no visible re-enforcement of the cavalry in Fairfax County from the front, but the line of picket posts was noticeably shortened.

About two weeks later, with forty men, Mosby raided a post at Herndon Station, bringing off a major, a captain, two lieutenants and twenty-one men, with a horse apiece. A week later, with fifty-odd men, he cut up about three times his strength of Union cavalry at Chantilly. Having surprised a small party, he had driven them into a much larger force, and the hunted had turned to hunt the hunters. Fighting a delaying action with a few men while the bulk of his force fell back on an old roadblock of felled trees dating from the second Manassas campaign, he held off the enemy until he was sure his ambuscade was set, then, by feigning headlong flight, led them into a trap and chased the survivors for five or six miles. Wyndham and Stoughton had found Mosby an annoying nuisance; their successors were finding him a serious menace.

This attitude was not confined to the local level, but extended all the way to the top echelons. The word passed down, "Get Mosby!" and it was understood that the officer responsible for his elimination would find his military career made for him. One of the Union officers who saw visions of rapid advancement over the wreckage of Mosby's Rangers was a captain of the First Vermont, Josiah Flint by name. He was soon to have a chance at it.

On March 31, Mosby's Rangers met at Middleburg and moved across the mountain to Chantilly, expecting to take a strong outpost which had been located there. On arriving, they found the campsite deserted. The post had been pulled back closer to Fairfax after the fight of four days before. Mosby decided to move up to the Potomac and attack a Union force on the other side of Dranesville – Captain Josiah Flint's Vermonters.

They passed the night at John Miskel's farm, near Chantilly. The following morning, April 1, at about daybreak, Mosby was wakened by one of his men who had been sleeping in the barn. This man, having gone outside, had observed a small party of Union troops on the Maryland side of the river who were making semaphore signals to somebody on the Virginia side. Mosby ordered everybody to turn out as quickly as possible and went out to watch the signalmen with his field glasses. While he was watching, Dick Moran, a Mosby man who had billeted with friends down the road, arrived at a breakneck gallop from across the fields, shouting: "Mount your horses! The Yankees are coming!"

It appeared that he had been wakened, shortly before, by the noise of a column of cavalry on the road in front of the house where he had been sleeping, and had seen a strong force of Union cavalry on the march in the direction of Broad Run and the Miskel farm. Waiting until they had passed, he had gotten his horse and circled at a gallop through the woods, reaching the farm just ahead of them. It later developed that a woman of the neighborhood, whose head had been turned by the attentions of Union officers, had betrayed Mosby to Flint.

The Miskel farmhouse stood on the crest of a low hill, facing the river. Behind it stood the big barn, with a large barnyard enclosed by a high pole fence. As this was a horse farm, all the fences were eight feet high and quite strongly built. A lane ran down the slope of the hill between two such fences, and at the southern end of the slope another fence separated the meadows from a belt of woods, beyond which was the road from Dranesville, along which Flint's column was advancing.

It was a nasty spot for Mosby. He had between fifty and sixty men, newly roused from sleep, their horses unsaddled, and he was penned in by strong fences which would have to be breached if he were to escape. His only hope lay in a prompt counterattack. The men who had come out of the house and barn were frantically saddling horses, without much attention to whose saddle went on whose mount. Harry Hatcher, who had gotten his horse saddled, gave it to Mosby and appropriated somebody else's mount.

As Flint, at the head of his cavalry, emerged from the woods, Mosby had about twenty of his men mounted and was ready to receive him. The Union cavalry paused, somebody pulled out the gate bars at the foot of the lane, and the whole force started up toward the farm. Having opened the barnyard end of the lane, Mosby waited until Flint had come about halfway, then gave him a blast of revolver fire and followed this with a headlong charge down the lane. Flint was killed at the first salvo, as were several of the men behind him. By the time Mosby's charge rammed into the head of the Union attack, the narrow lane was blocked with riderless horses, preventing each force from coming to grips with the other. Here Mosby's insistence upon at least two revolvers for each man paid off, as did the target practice upon which he was always willing to expend precious ammunition. The Union column, constricted by the fences on either side of the lane and shaken by the death of their leader and by the savage attack of men whom they had believed hopelessly trapped, turned and tried to retreat, but when they reached the foot of the lane it was discovered that some fool, probably meaning to deny Mosby an avenue of escape, had replaced the gatebars. By this time, the rest of Mosby's force had mounted their horses, breaches had been torn in the fence at either side of the lane, and there were Confederates in both meadows, firing into the trapped men. Until the gate at the lower end gave way under the weight of horses crowded against it, there was a bloody slaughter. Within a few minutes Flint and nine of his men were killed, some fifteen more were given disabling wounds, eighty-two prisoners were taken, and over a hundred horses and large quantities of arms and ammunition were captured. The remains of Flint's force was chased as far as Dranesville. Mosby was still getting the prisoners sorted out, rounding up loose horses, gathering weapons and ammunition from casualties, and giving the wounded first aid, when a Union lieutenant rode up under a flag of truce, followed by several enlisted men and two civilians of the Sanitary Commission, the Civil War equivalent of the Red Cross, to pick up the wounded and bury the dead. This officer offered to care for Mosby's wounded with his own, an offer which was declined with thanks. Mosby said he would carry his casualties with him, and the Union officer could scarcely believe his eyes when he saw only three wounded men on horse litters and one dead man tied to his saddle.

The sutlers at Dranesville had heard the firing and were about to move away when Mosby's column appeared. Seeing the preponderance of blue uniforms, they mistook the victors for prisoners and, anticipating a lively and profitable business, unpacked their loads and set up their counters. The business was lively, but anything but profitable. The Mosby men looted them unmercifully, taking their money, their horses, and everything else they had.

All through the spring of 1863, Mosby kept jabbing at Union lines of communication in northern Virginia. In June, his majority came through, and with it authority to organize a battalion under the Scott Law. From that time on, he was on his own, and there was no longer any danger of his being recalled to the regular Army. He was responsible only to Jeb Stuart until the general's death at Yellow Tavern a year later; thereafter, he took orders from no source below General Lee and the Secretary of War.

Even before this regularization of status, Mosby's force was beginning to look like a regular outfit. From the fifteen men he had brought up from Culpepper in mid-January, its effective and dependable strength had grown to about sixty riders, augmented from raid to raid by the "Conglomerate" fringe, who were now accepted as guerrillas-pro-tem without too much enthusiasm. A new type of recruit had begun to appear, the man who came to enlist on a permanent basis. Some were Maryland secessionists, like James Williamson, who, after the war, wrote an authoritative and well-documented history of the organization, Mosby's Rangers. Some were boys like John Edmonds and John Munson, who had come of something approaching military age since the outbreak of the war. Some were men who had wangled transfers from other Confederate units. Not infrequently these men had given up commissions in the regular army to enlist as privates with Mosby. For example, there was the former clergyman, Sam Chapman, who had been a captain of artillery, or the Prussian uhlan lieutenant, Baron Robert von Massow, who gave up a captaincy on Stuart's staff, or the Englishman, Captain Hoskins, who was shortly to lose his life because of his preference for the saber over the revolver, or Captain Bill Kennon, late of Wheat's Louisiana Tigers, who had also served with Walker in Nicaragua. As a general thing, the new Mosby recruit was a man of high intelligence, reckless bravery and ultra-rugged individualism.

For his home territory, Mosby now chose a rough quadrangle between the Blue Ridge and Bull Run Mountain, bounded at its four corners by Snicker's Gap and Manassas Gap along the former and Thoroughfare Gap and Aldie Gap along the latter. Here, when not in action, the Mosby men billeted themselves, keeping widely dispersed, and an elaborate system, involving most of the inhabitants, free or slave, was set up to transmit messages, orders and warnings. In time this district came to be known as "Mosby's Confederacy," and, in the absence of any effective Confederate States civil authority, Mosby became the lawgiver and chief magistrate as well as military commander. John Munson, who also wrote a book of reminiscences after the war, said that Mosby's Confederacy was an absolute monarchy, and that none was ever better governed in history.

Adhering to his belief in the paramount importance of firepower, Mosby saw to it that none of his men carried fewer than two revolvers, and the great majority carried four, one pair on the belt and another on the saddle. Some extremists even carried a third pair down their boot-tops, giving them thirty-six shots without reloading. Nor did he underestimate the power of mobility. Each man had his string of horses, kept where they could be picked up at need. Unlike the regular cavalryman with his one mount, a Mosby man had only to drop an exhausted animal at one of these private remount stations and change his saddle to a fresh one. As a result of these two practices, Union combat reports throughout the war consistently credited Mosby with from three to five times his actual strength.

In time, the entire economy of Mosby's Confederacy came to be geared to Mosby's operations, just as the inhabitants of seventeenth century Tortugas or Port Royal depended for their livelihood on the loot of the buccaneers. The Mosby man who lived with some farmer's family paid for his lodging with gifts of foodstuffs and blankets looted from the enemy. There was always a brisk trade in captured U. S. Army horses and mules. And there was a steady flow of United States currency into the section, so that in time Confederate money was driven out of circulation in a sort of reversal of Gresham's law. Every prisoner taken reasonably close to Army pay day could be counted on for a few dollars, and in each company there would be some lucky or skillful gambler who would have a fairly sizeable roll of greenbacks. And, of course, there was the sutler, the real prize catch; any Mosby man would pass up a general in order to capture a sutler.

And Northern-manufactured goods filtered south by the wagonload. Many of the Mosby men wore Confederate uniforms that had been tailored for them in Baltimore and even in Washington and run through the Union lines.

By mid-June, Lee's invasion of Pennsylvania had begun and the countryside along Bull Run Mountain and the Blue Ridge exploded into a series of cavalry actions as the Confederate Army moved north along the Union right. Mosby kept his little force out of the main fighting, hacking away at the Union troops from behind and confusing their combat intelligence with reports of Rebel cavalry appearing where none ought to be. In the midst of this work, he took time out to dash across into Fairfax County with sixty men, shooting up a wagon train, burning wagons, and carrying off prisoners and mules, the latter being turned over to haul Lee's invasion transport. After the two armies had passed over the Potomac, he gathered his force and launched an invasion of Pennsylvania on his own, getting as far as Mercersburg and bringing home a drove of over 200 beef cattle.

He got back to Mosby's Confederacy in time to learn of Lee's defeat at Gettysburg. Realizing that Lee's retreat would be followed by a pursuing Union army, he began making preparations to withstand the coming deluge. For one thing, he decided to do something he had not done before – concentrate his force in a single camp on the top of Bull Run Mountain. In the days while Lee's army was trudging southward, Mosby gathered every horse and mule and cow he could find and drove them into the mountains, putting boys and slaves to work herding them. He commandeered wagons, and hauled grain and hay to his temporary camp. His men erected huts, and built corrals for horses and a stockade for prisoners. They even moved a blacksmith shop to the hidden camp. Then Mosby sat down and waited.

A few days later, Meade's army began coming through. The Forty-Third Partisan Ranger Battalion went to work immediately. For two weeks, they galloped in and out among the Union columns, returning to their hidden camp only long enough to change horses and leave the prisoners they had taken. They cut into wagon trains, scattering cavalry escorts, burning wagons, destroying supplies, blowing up ammunition, disabling cannon, running off mules. They ambushed marching infantry, flitting away before their victims had recovered from the initial surprise. Sometimes, fleeing from the scene of one attack, they would burst through a column on another road, leaving confusion behind to delay the pursuit.

Finally, the invaders passed on, the camp on the mountain top was abandoned, the Mosby men went back to their old billets, and the Forty-Third Battalion could take it easy again. That is to say, they only made a raid every couple of days and seldom fought a pitched battle more than once a week.

The summer passed; the Virginia hills turned from green to red and from red to brown. Mosby was severely wounded in the side and thigh during a fight at Gooding's Tavern on August 23, when two of his men were killed, but the raiders brought off eighty-five horses and twelve prisoners and left six enemy dead behind. The old days of bloodless sneak raids on isolated picket posts were past, now that they had enough men for two companies and Mosby rarely took the field with fewer than a hundred riders behind him.

Back in the saddle again after recovering from his wounds, Mosby devoted more attention to attacking the Orange and Alexandria and the

Manassas Gap railroads and to harassing attacks for the rest of the winter.

In January, 1864, Major Cole, of the Union Maryland cavalry, began going out of his way to collide with the Forty-Third Virginia, the more so since he had secured the services of a deserter from Mosby, a man named Binns who had been expelled from the Rangers for some piece of rascality and was thirsting for revenge. Cole hoped to capitalize on Binns' defection as Mosby had upon the desertion of Sergeant Ames, and he made several raids into Mosby's Confederacy, taking a number of prisoners before the Mosby men learned the facts of the situation and everybody found a new lodging place.

On the morning of February 20, Mosby was having breakfast at a farmhouse near Piedmont Depot, on the Manassas Gap Railroad, along with John Munson and John Edmonds, the 'teen-age terrors, and a gunsmith named Jake Lavender, who was the battalion ordnance sergeant and engaged to young Edmonds' sister. Edmonds had with him a couple of Sharps carbines he had repaired for other members of the battalion and was carrying to return to the owners. Suddenly John Edmonds' younger brother, Jimmy, burst into the room with the news that several hundred Union cavalrymen were approaching. Lavender grabbed the two carbines, for which he had a quantity of ammunition, and they all ran outside.

Sending the younger Edmonds boy to bring re-enforcements, Mosby, accompanied by John Edmonds, Munson, and Jake Lavender, started to follow the enemy. He and Munson each took one of Lavender's carbines and opened fire on them, Munson killing a horse and Mosby a man. That started things off properly. Cole's Marylanders turned and gave chase, and Mosby led them toward the rendezvous with Jimmy Edmonds and the re-enforcements. Everybody arrived together, Mosby's party, the pursuers, and the re-enforcements, and a running fight ensued, with Cole's men running ahead. This mounted chase, in the best horse-opera manner, came thundering down a road past a schoolhouse just as the pupils were being let out for recess. One of these, a 14-year-old boy named Cabell Maddox, jumped onto the pony on which he had ridden to school and joined in the pursuit, armed only with a McGuffy's Third Reader. Overtaking a fleeing Yank, he aimed the book at him and demanded his surrender; before the flustered soldier realized that his captor was unarmed, the boy had snatched the Colt from his belt and was covering him in earnest. This marked the suspension, for the duration of hostilities, of young Maddox's formal education. From that hour on he was a Mosby man, and he served with distinction to the end of the war.

The chase broke off, finally, when the pursuers halted to get their prisoners and captured horses together. Then they discovered that one of their number, a man named Cobb, had been killed. Putting the dead man across his saddle, they carried the body back to Piedmont, and the next day assembled there for the funeral. The services had not yet started, and Mosby was finishing writing a report to Stuart on the previous day's action, when a scout came pelting in to report Union cavalry in the vicinity of Middleburg.

Leaving the funeral in the hands of the preacher and the civilian mourners, Mosby and the 150 men who had assembled mounted and started off. Sam Chapman, the ex-artillery captain, who had worked up from the ranks to a lieutenancy with Mosby, was left in charge of the main force, while Mosby and a small party galloped ahead to reconnoiter. The enemy, they discovered, were not Cole's men but a California battalion. They learned that this force had turned in the direction of Leesburg, and that they were accompanied by the deserter, Binns.

Mosby made up his mind to ambush the Californians on their way back to their camp at Vienna. He had plans, involving a length of rope, for his former trooper, Binns. The next morning, having crossed Bull Run Mountain the night before, he took up a position near Dranesville, with scouts out to the west. When the enemy were finally reported approaching, he was ready for them. Twenty of his 150, with carbines and rifles, were dismounted and placed in the center, under Lieutenant Mountjoy. The rest of the force was divided into two equal sections, under Chapman and Frank Williams, and kept mounted on the flanks. Mosby himself took his place with Williams on the right. While they waited, they could hear the faint boom of cannon from Washington, firing salutes in honor of Washington's Birthday.

A couple of men, posted in advance, acted as decoys, and the Union cavalry, returning empty-handed from their raid, started after them in hopes of bringing home at least something to show for their efforts. Before they knew it, they were within range of Mountjoy's concealed riflemen. While they were still in disorder from the surprise volley, the two mounted sections swept in on them in a blaze of revolver fire, and they broke and fled. There was a nasty jam in a section of fenced road, with mounted Mosby men in the woods on either side and Mountjoy's rifles behind them. Before they could get clear of this, they lost fifteen killed, fifteen more wounded, and over seventy prisoners, and the victorious Mosby men brought home over a hundred captured horses and large quantities of arms and ammunition. To their deep regret, however, Binns was not to be found either among the casualties or the prisoners. As soon as he had seen how the fight was going, the deserter had spurred off northward, never to appear in Virginia again. Mosby's own loss had been one man killed and four wounded.

For the rest of the spring, operations were routine – attacks on wagon trains and train wrecking and bridge burning on the railroads. With the cut-and-try shifting of command of the Union Army of the Potomac over and Grant in command, there was activity all over northern Virginia. About this time, Mosby got hold of a second twelve-pound howitzer, and, later, a twelve-pound Napoleon and added the Shenandoah Valley to his field of operations.

From then on, Mosby was fighting a war on two fronts, dividing his attention between the valley and the country to the east of Bull Run Mountain, his men using their spare horses freely to keep the Union rear on both sides in an uproar. The enemy, knowing the section from whence Mosby was operating, resorted to frequent counter-raiding. Often, returning from a raid, the Mosby men would find their home territory invaded and would have to intercept or fight off the invaders. At this time, Mosby was giving top priority to attacks on Union transport whether on the roads or the railroads. Wagon trains were in constant movement, both moving up the Shenandoah Valley and bound for the Army of the Potomac, in front of Petersburg. To the east was the Orange and Alexandria Railroad, to the south, across the end of Mosby's Confederacy, was the Manassas Gap, and at the upper end of the valley was the B. & O. The section of the Manassas Gap Railroad along the southern boundary of Mosby's Confederacy came in for special attention, and the Union Army finally gave it up for a bad job and abandoned it. This writer's grandfather, Captain H. B. Piper, of the Eleventh Pennsylvania Volunteer Infantry, did a stint of duty guarding it, and until he died he spoke with respect of the abilities of John S. Mosby and his raiders. Locomotives were knocked out with one or another of Mosby's twelve-pounders. Track was torn up and bridges were burned. Land-mines were planted. Trains were derailed and looted, usually with sharp fighting.

By mid-July, Mosby had been promoted to lieutenant colonel and had a total strength of around 300 men, divided into five companies. His younger brother, William Mosby, had joined him and was acting as his adjutant. He now had four guns, all twelve-pounders – two howitzers, the Napoleon and a new rifle, presented to him by Jubal Early. He had a compact, well-disciplined and powerful army-in-miniature. After the Union defeat at Kernstown, Early moved back to the lower end of the Shenandoah Valley, and McCausland went off on his raid in to Pennsylvania, burning Chambersburg in retaliation for Hunter's burnings at Lexington and Buchanan in Virginia. Following his customary practice, Mosby made a crossing at another point and raided into Maryland as far as Adamstown, skirmishing and picking up a few prisoners and horses.

Early's invasion of Maryland, followed as it was by McCausland's sack of Chambersburg, was simply too much for the Union command. The Shenandoah situation had to be cleaned up immediately, and, after some top-echelon dickering, Grant picked Phil Sheridan to do the cleaning. On August 7, Sheridan assumed command of the heterogeneous Union forces in the Shenandoah and began welding them into an army. On the 10th, he started south after Early, and Mosby, who generally had a good idea of what was going on at Union headquarters, took a small party into the valley, intending to kidnap the new commander as he had Stoughton. Due mainly to the vigilance of a camp sentry, the plan failed, but Mosby picked up the news that a large wagon train was being sent up the valley, and he decided to have a try at this.

On the evening of the 12th, he was back in the valley with 330 men and his two howitzers. Spending the night at a plantation on the right bank of the Shenandoah River, he was on the move before daybreak, crossing the river and pushing toward Berryville, with scouts probing ahead in the heavy fog. One of the howitzers broke a wheel and was pushed into the brush and left behind. As both pieces were of the same caliber, the caisson was taken along. A lieutenant and fifteen men, scouting ahead, discovered a small empty wagon train, going down the valley in the direction of Harper's Ferry, and they were about to attack it when they heard, in the distance, the rumbling of many heavily loaded wagons. This was the real thing. They forgot about the empty wagons and hastened back to Mosby and the main force to report.

Swinging to the left to avoid premature contact with the train, Mosby hurried his column in the direction of Berryville. On the way, he found a disabled wagon, part of the north-bound empty train, with the teamster and several infantrymen sleeping in it. These were promptly secured, and questioning elicited the information that the south-bound train consisted of 150 wagons, escorted by 250 cavalry and a brigade of infantry. Getting into position on a low hill overlooking the road a little to the east of Berryville, the howitzer was unlimbered and the force was divided on either side of it, Captain Adolphus Richards taking the left wing and Sam Chapman the right. Mosby himself remained with the gun. Action was to be commenced with the gun, and the third shot was to be the signal for both Richards and Chapman to charge.

At just the right moment, the fog lifted. The gun was quickly laid on the wagon train and fired, the first shot beheading a mule. The second shell hit the best sort of target imaginable – a mobile farrier's forge. There was a deadly shower of horseshoes, hand-tools and assorted ironmongery, inflicting casualties and causing a local panic. The third shell landed among some cavalry who were galloping up, scattering them, and, on the signal, Richards and Chapman charged simultaneously.

Some infantry at the head of the train met Richards with a volley, costing him one man killed and several wounded and driving his charge off at an angle into the middle of the train. The howitzer, in turn, broke up the infantry. Chapman, who had hit the rear of the train, was having easier going: his men methodically dragged the teamsters from their wagons, unhitched mules, overturned, looted and burned wagons. The bulk of the escort, including the infantry, were at the front of the train, with Richards' men between them and Chapman. Richards, while he had his hands full with these, was not neglecting the wagons, either, though he was making less of a ceremony of it. A teamster was shot and dragged from his wagon-seat, a lighted bundle of inflammables tossed into the wagon, and pistols were fired around the mules' heads to start them running. The faster they ran, the more the flames behind them were fanned, and as the wagon went careening down the road, other wagons were ignited by it.

By 8 a. m., the whole thing was over. The escort had been scattered, the wagons were destroyed, and the victors moved off, in possession of 500-odd mules, thirty-six horses, about 200 head of beef cattle, 208 prisoners, four Negro slaves who had been forcibly emancipated to drive Army wagons, and large quantities of supplies. In one of the wagons, a number of violins, probably equipment for some prototype of the U.S.O., were found; the more musically inclined guerrillas appropriated these and enlivened the homeward march with music.

Of course, there was jubilation all over Mosby's Confederacy on their return. The mules were herded into the mountains, held for about a week, and then started off for Early's army. The beef herd was divided among the people, and there were barbecues and feasts. A shadow was cast over the spirits of the raiders, however, when the prisoners informed them, with considerable glee, that the train had been carrying upwards of a million dollars, the pay for Sheridan's army. Even allowing for exaggeration, the fact that they had overlooked this treasure was a bitter pill for the Mosbyites. According to local tradition, however, the fortune was not lost completely; there were stories of a Berryville family who had been quite poor before the war but who blossomed into unexplained affluence afterward.

Less than a week later, on August 19, Mosby was in the valley again with 250 men, dividing his force into several parties after crossing the river at Castleman's Ford. Richards, with "B" Company, set off toward Charlestown. Mosby himself took "A" toward Harper's Ferry on an uneventful trip during which the only enemies he encountered were a couple of stragglers caught pillaging a springhouse. It was Chapman, with "C" and "D," who saw the action on this occasion.

Going to the vicinity of Berryville, he came to a burning farmhouse, and learned that it had been fired only a few minutes before by some of Custer's cavalry. Leaving a couple of men to help the family control the fire and salvage their possessions, he pressed on rapidly. Here was the thing every Mosby man had been hoping for – a chance to catch house burners at work. They passed a second blazing house and barn, dropping off a couple more men to help fight fire, and caught up with the incendiaries, a company of Custer's men, just as they were setting fire to a third house. Some of these, knowing the quality of mercy they might expect from Mosby men, made off immediately at a gallop. About ninety of them, however, tried to form ranks and put up a fight. The fight speedily became a massacre. Charging with shouts of "No quarters!," Chapman's men drove them into a maze of stone fences and killed about a third of them before the rest were able to extricate themselves.

This didn't stop the house burnings, by any means. The devastation of the Shenandoah Valley had been decided upon as a matter of strategy, and Sheridan was going through with it. The men who were ordered to do the actual work did not have their morale improved any by the knowledge that Mosby's Rangers were refusing quarter to incendiary details, however, and, coming as it did on the heels of the wagon train affair of the 13th, Sheridan was convinced that something drastic would have to be done about Mosby. Accordingly, he set up a special company, under a Captain William Blazer, each man armed with a pair of revolvers and a Spencer repeater, to devote their entire efforts to eliminating Mosby and his organized raiders.

On September 3, this company caught up with Joe Nelson and about 100 men in the valley and gave them a sound drubbing, the first that the Mosby men had experienced for some time. It was a humiliating defeat for them, and, on the other side, it was hailed as the beginning of the end of the Mosby nuisance. A few days later, while raiding to the east of Bull Run Mountain, Mosby was wounded again, and was taken to Lynchburg. He was joined by his wife, who remained with him at Lynchburg and at Mosby's Confederacy until the end of the war.

During his absence, the outfit seems to have been run by a sort of presidium of the senior officers. On September 22, Sam Chapman took 120 men into the valley to try to capture a cavalry post supposed to be located near Front Royal, but, arriving there, he learned that his information had been incorrect and that no such post existed. Camping in the woods, he sent some men out as scouts, and the next morning they reported a small wagon train escorted by about 150 cavalry, moving toward Front Royal. Dividing his force and putting half of it under Walter Frankland, he planned to attack the train from the rear while Frankland hit it from in front. After getting into position, he kept his men concealed, waiting for the wagons to pass, and as it did, he realized that his scouts had seen only a small part of it. The escort looked to him like about three regiments. Ordering his men to slip away as quietly as possible, he hurried to reach Frankland.

"Turn around, Walter!" he yelled. "Get your men out of here! You're attacking a whole brigade!"

"What of it?" Frankland replied. "Why, Sam, we have the bastards on the run already!"

Chapman, the erstwhile clergyman, turned loose a blast of theological language in purely secular connotation. Frankland, amazed at this blasphemous clamor from his usually pious comrade, realized that it must have been inspired by something more than a little serious, and began ordering his men to fall back. Before they had all gotten away, two of the three Union regiments accompanying the wagons came galloping up and swamped them. Most of the men got away but six of them, Anderson, Carter, Overby, Love, Rhodes and Jones, were captured.

Late that night some of the stragglers, making their way back to Mosby's Confederacy on foot, reported the fate of these six men. They had been taken into Front Royal, and there, at the personal order of General George A. Custer, and under circumstances of extreme brutality, they had all been hanged. Rhodes' mother, who lived in Front Royal, had been forced to witness the hanging of her son.

To put it conservatively, there was considerable excitement in Mosby's Confederacy when the news of this atrocity was received. The senior officers managed to restore a measure of calmness, however, and it was decided to wait until Mosby returned before taking any action on the matter.

In addition to the hangings at Front Royal, Custer was acquiring a bad reputation because of his general brutality to the people of the Shenandoah Valley. After the battle of the Little Bighorn, Sitting Bull would have probably won any popularity contest in northern Virginia without serious competition.

On September 29, Mosby was back with his command; his wound had not been as serious as it might have been for the bullet had expended most of its force against the butt of one of the revolvers in his belt. Operations against the railroads had been allowed to slacken during Mosby's absence; now they were stepped up again. Track was repeatedly torn up along the Manassas Gap line, and there were attacks on camps and strong points, and continual harassing of wood-cutting parties obtaining fuel for the locomotives. The artillery was taken out, and trains were shelled. All this, of course, occasioned a fresh wave of Union raids into the home territory of the raiders, during one of which Yank Ames, who had risen to a lieutenancy in the Forty-Third, was killed.

The most desperate efforts were being made, at this time, to keep the Manassas Gap Railroad open, and General C. C. Augur, who had charge of the railroad line at the time, was arresting citizens indiscriminately and forcing them to ride on the trains as hostages. Mosby obtained authorization from Lee's headquarters to use reprisal measures on officers and train crews of trains on which citizens were being forced to ride, and also authority to execute prisoners from Custer's command in equal number to the men hanged at Front Royal and elsewhere.

It was not until November that he was able to secure prisoners from Custer's brigade, it being his intention to limit his retaliation to men from units actually involved in the hangings. On November 6, he paraded about twenty-five such prisoners and forced them to draw lots, selecting, in this manner, seven of them – one for each of the men hanged at Front Royal and another for a man named Willis who had been hanged at Gaines' Cross Roads several weeks later. It was decided that they should be taken into the Shenandoah Valley and hanged beside the Valley Pike, where their bodies could serve as an object lesson. On the way, one of them escaped. Four were hanged, and then, running out of rope, they prepared to shoot the other two. One of these got away during a delay caused by defective percussion caps on his executioner's revolver.

A sign was placed over the bodies, setting forth the reason for their execution, and Mosby also sent one of his men under a flag of truce to

Sheridan's headquarters, with a statement of what had been done and why, re-enforced with the intimation that he had more prisoners, including a number of officers, in case his messenger failed to return safely. Sheridan replied by disclaiming knowledge of the Front Royal hangings, agreeing that Mosby was justified in taking reprisals, and assuring the Confederate leader that hereafter his men would be given proper treatment as prisoners of war. There was no repetition of the hangings.

By this time the Shenandoah Valley campaign as such was over. The last Confederate effort to clear Sheridan out of the Valley had failed at Cedar Creek on October 19, and the victor was going methodically about his task of destroying the strategic and economic usefulness of the valley. How well he succeeded in this was best expressed in Sheridan's own claim that a crow flying over the region would have to carry his own rations. The best Mosby could do was to launch small raiding parties to harass the work of destruction.

By the beginning of December, the northern or Loudoun County end of Mosby's Confederacy was feeling the enemy scourge as keenly as the valley, and the winter nights were lighted with the flames of burning houses and barns. For about a week, while this was going on, Mosby abandoned any attempt at organized action. His men, singly and in small parties, darted in and out among the invaders, sniping and bushwhacking, attacking when they could and fleeing when they had to, and taking no prisoners. When it was over, the northern end of Mosby's Confederacy was in ashes and most of the people had "refugeed out," but Mosby's Rangers, as a fighting force, was still intact. On December 17, for instance, while Mosby was in Richmond conferring with General Lee, they went into the valley again in force, waylaying a column of cavalry on the march, killing and wounding about thirty and bringing off 168 prisoners and horses.

When Mosby came back from Lee's headquarters, a full colonel now, his brother William was made a lieutenant-colonel, and Richards became a major. The southern, or Fauquier County, end of Mosby's Confederacy was still more or less intact, though crowded with refugees. There was even time, in spite of everything, for the wedding of the Forty-Third's armorer, Jake Lavender, with John and Jimmy Edmonds' sister.

While the wedding party was in progress, a report was brought in to the effect that Union cavalry were in the neighborhood of Salem, a few miles away. Mosby took one of his men, Tom Love, a relative of one of the Front Royal victims, and went to investigate, finding that the enemy had moved in the direction of Rectortown, where they were making camp for the night. Sending a resident of the neighborhood to alert

Chapman and Richards for an attack at daybreak, Mosby and Love set out to collect others of his command.

By this time, it was dark, with a freezing rain covering everything with ice. Mosby and Love decided to stop at the farm of Ludwell Lake for something to eat before going on; Love wanted to stay outside on guard, but Mosby told him to get off his horse and come inside. As they would have been in any house in the neighborhood, Mosby and his companion were welcomed as honored guests and sat down with the family to a hearty meal of spareribs.

While they were eating, the house was surrounded by Union cavalry. Mosby rushed to the back door, to find the backyard full of soldiers. He started for the front door, but as he did, it burst open and a number of Yankees, officers and men, entered the house. At the same time, the soldiers behind, having seen the back door open and shut, began firing at the rear windows, and one bullet hit Mosby in the abdomen. In the confusion, with the women of the Lake family screaming, the soldiers cursing, and bullets coming through the windows, the kitchen table was overturned and the lights extinguished. Mosby in the dark, managed to crawl into a first-floor bedroom, where he got off his tell-tale belt and coat, stuffing them under the bed. Then he lay down on the floor.

After a while, the shooting outside stopped, the officers returned, and the candles were relighted. The Union officers found Mosby on the floor, bleeding badly, and asked the family who he was. They said, of course, that they did not know, and neither did Tom Love – he was only a Confederate officer on his way to rejoin his command, who had stopped for a night's lodging. There was a surgeon with the Union detachment. After they got most of Mosby's clothes off and put him on the bed, he examined the wounded Confederate and pronounced his wound mortal. When asked his name and unit, Mosby, still conscious, hastily improvised a false identity, at the same time congratulating himself on having left all his documents behind when starting on this scouting trip. Having been assured, by medical authority, that he was as good as dead, the Union officers were no longer interested in him and soon went away.

Fortunately, on his visit to Lee's headquarters, Mosby had met an old schoolmate, a Dr. Montiero, who was now a surgeon with the Confederate Army, and, persuading him to get a transfer, had brought him back with him. Montiero's new C.O. was his first patient in his new outfit. Early the next morning, he extracted the bullet. The next night Mosby was taken to Lynchburg.

Despite the Union doctor's pronouncement of his impending death, Mosby was back in action again near the end of February, 1865. His return was celebrated with another series of raids on both sides of the mountains. It was, of course, obvious to everybody that the sands of the Confederacy were running out, but the true extent of the debacle was somewhat obscured to Mosby's followers by their own immediate successes. Peace rumors began drifting about, the favorite item of wish-thinking being that the Union government was going to recognize the Confederacy and negotiate a peace in return for Confederate help in throwing the French out of Mexico. Of course, Mosby himself never believed any such nonsense, but he continued his attacks as though victory were just around the corner. On April 5, two days after the Union army entered Richmond, a party of fifty Mosby men caught their old enemies, the Loudoun Rangers, in camp near Halltown and beat them badly. On April 9, the day of Lee's surrender, "D" Company and the newly organized "H" Company fired the last shots for the Forty-Third Virginia in a skirmish in Fairfax County. Two days later, Mosby received a message from General Hancock, calling for his surrender.

He sent a group of his officers – William Mosby, Sam Chapman, Walter Frankland and Dr. Montiero – with a flag of truce, and, after several other meetings with Hancock, the command was disbanded and most of the men went in to take the parole.

When his armistice with Hancock expired, Mosby found himself with only about forty irreconcilables left out of his whole command. As General Joe Johnston had not yet surrendered, he did not feel justified in getting out of the fight, himself. With his bloodied but unbowed handful, he set out on the most ambitious project of his entire military career – nothing less than a plan to penetrate into Richmond and abduct General Grant. If this scheme succeeded, it was his intention to dodge around the Union Army, carry his distinguished prisoner to Johnston, and present him with a real bargaining point for negotiating terms.

They reached the outskirts of Richmond and made a concealed camp across the river, waiting for darkness. In the meanwhile, two of the party, both natives of the city, Munson and Cole Jordan, went in to scout. Several hours passed, and neither returned. Mosby feared that they had been picked up by Union patrols. He was about to send an older man, Lieutenant Ben Palmer, when a canal-boat passed, and, hailing it, they learned of Johnston's surrender.

That was the end of the scheme to kidnap Grant. As long as a Confederate force was still under arms, it would have been a legitimate act of war. Now, it would be mere brigandage, and Mosby had no intention of turning brigand.

So Mosby returned to Fauquier County to take the parole. For him, the fighting was over, but he was soon to discover that the war was not. At that time, Edwin M. Stanton was making frantic efforts to inculpate as many prominent Confederates as possible in the Booth conspiracy, and Mosby's name was suggested as a worthy addition to Stanton's long and fantastic list of alleged conspirators. A witness was produced to testify that Mosby had been in Washington on the night of the assassination, April 14. At that time, Stanton was able to produce a witness to almost anything he wanted to establish. Fortunately, Mosby had an alibi; at the time in question, he had been at Hancock's headquarters, discussing armistice terms; even Stanton couldn't get around that.

However, he was subjected to considerable petty persecution, and once he was flung into jail without charge and held incommunicado. His wife went to Washington to plead his case before President Johnson, who treated her with a great deal less than courtesy, and then before General Grant, who promptly gave her a written order for her husband's release.

Then, in 1868, he did something which would have been social and political suicide for any Southerner with a less imposing war record. He supported Ulysses S. Grant for President. It was about as unexpected as any act in an extremely unconventional career, and, as usual, he had a well-reasoned purpose. Grant, he argued, was a professional soldier, not a politician. His enmity toward the South had been confined to the battlefield and had ended with the war. He had proven his magnanimity to the defeated enemy, and as President, he could be trusted to show fairness and clemency to the South.

While Virginia had not voted in the election of 1868, there is no question that Mosby's declaration of support helped Grant, and Grant was grateful, inviting Mosby to the White House after his inauguration and later appointing him to the United States consulate at Hong Kong. After the expiration of his consular service, Mosby resumed his law practice, eventually taking up residence in Washington. He found time to write several books – war reminiscences and memoirs, and a volume in vindication of his former commander, Jeb Stuart, on the Confederate cavalry in the Gettysburg campaign. He died in Washington, at the age of eighty-three, in 1916.

The really important part of John Mosby's career, of course, was the two years and three months, from January, 1863, to April, 1865, in which he held independent command. With his tiny force – it never exceeded 500 men – he had compelled the Union army to employ at least one and often as high as three brigades to guard against his depredations, and these men, held in the rear, were as much out of the war proper as though they had been penned up in Andersonville or Libby Prison.

In addition to this, every northward movement of the Confederate Army after January, 1863, was accompanied by a diversionary operation of Mosby's command, sometimes tactically insignificant but always contributing, during the critical time of the operation, to the uncertainty of Union intelligence. Likewise, every movement to the south of the Army of the Potomac was harassed from behind.

It may also be noted that Sheridan, quite capable of dealing with the menace of Stuart, proved helpless against the Mosby nuisance, although, until they were wiped out, Blazer's Scouts were the most efficient anti-Mosby outfit ever employed. In spite of everything that was done against them, however, Mosby's Rangers stayed in business longer than Lee's army, and when they finally surrendered, it was not because they, themselves, had been defeated, but because the war had been literally jerked out from under them.

Mosby made the cavalry a formidable amalgamation of fire power and mobility and his influence on military history was felt directly, and survived him by many years. In his last days, while living in Washington, the old Confederate guerrilla had a youthful friend, a young cavalry lieutenant fresh from West Point, to whom he enjoyed telling the stories of his raids and battles and to whom he preached his gospel of fire and mobility. This young disciple of Mosby's old age was to make that gospel his own, and to practice it, later, with great success. The name of this young officer was George S. Patton, Jr. – H. Beam Piper

The End

www.ingramcontent.com/pod-product-compliance
Lightning Source LLC
Chambersburg PA
CBHW030418310726
48979CB00007B/1105

* 9 7 8 1 6 0 3 1 2 9 3 2 9 *